The Ink Returns!

The Whitlock Inheritance

Book 2: Haven Cove Series

Sonia D. Hebdon

Paperback: ISBN: 978-1-7641056-2-0

eBook ISBN: 978-1-7641056-3-7

"First Edition: December 2025" AUSTRALIA
Book 2: Haven Cove Series "The Ink Returns: The Whitlock Inheritance"

Copyright © Cover Design J.F.E. Marshall
Illustrations created with Recraft AI art.

Edited by A.E. Marshall

Publisher: J.F.E. Marshall.

Description: The Ink Returns. The Whitlock Inheritance. Sonia D. Hebdon.

Audience: Teens and Young Adults aged 13—25 years, 6 x 9 inches, 247 pages, black and white with illustrations.

<u>*DEDICATION*</u>

To Morgan Thompson, my beautiful, shining cousin, whose radiant spirit left this world far too soon; your memory is a bright star guiding my way.

And to my dear friend Jason Heart, whose passion for fantasy ignites dreams in my mind and whose steadfast presence, like a gentle lighthouse in the distance, has always illuminated my path. Thank you, from the depths of my soul, for your friendship and inspiration over the past thirty-five years.

The Whitlock Estate,

Los Angeles

CONTENTS

<u>Sonia D. Hebdon's Other Titles</u>

<u>Parenting ASD and DID children</u>

The Crazy Mother's Guide To Raising Exceptional Children. An Aussie Mum's First-Hand Experience Parenting Children Who Have Autism Spectrum Disorder and Dissociative Identity Disorder.

Early readers for children with ASD (Autism Spectrum Disorder)

<u>I Am Perfect The Way I Am Series</u>

Book 1 Vlad McCoy, A Unique Vampire Boy

Book 2 I Am A Superhero

Book 3 Ruby Ray Is Only A Dream Away!

YA Dark Romance, Paranormal Romance, Urban Fantasy, Clean Fiction for teens
<u>Faith-Infused Fiction</u>

<u>Haven Cove Series</u>

Book 1 Sincerely Yours ... Written In The Stars And Inked In Destiny!

Book 2 The Ink Returns! The Whitlock Inheritance.

Book 3 Scheduled for release in July 2026.

BLAINE'S ARTISTIC
INSPIRATION SIDE A

"It's the end of the world" REM
"Dance Hall Days," Wang Chung
"Head Over Heels" Go-Go's
"Heart Break Beat"
The Psychedelic Furs
"If You Were Here"
The Thompson Twins
"Sweet Dreams" Eurythmics
"I Could Be Happy"
Altered Images
"The Mirror Man"
Human League
"Feels Like Heaven"
Fiction Factory
"Melt With You" Modern English
"Halfway To Crazy" Jesus and
The Mary Chain

BLAINE'S ARTISTIC
INSPIRATION SIDE B

"The Promise" When In Rome
"Behind The Wheel" Depeche
Mode
"Love Song" The Cure
"The Riddle" Nik Kershaw
"Don't Fear The Reaper"
Blue Öyster Cult
"Ghost In You" The Psychedelic
Furs
"Ship Of Fools" World Party
"Compulsion" Martin Gore
"Wild Child" Iggy Pop
"Cuts You Up" Peter Murphy
"Bring On The Dancing Horses"
Echo & The Bunnymen
"Human" The Human League
"Atmosphere" Joy Division

The Ink Returns! The Whitlock Chronicles Soundtrack is now available on Spotify.

https://open.spotify.com/playlist/7uT49UtREEm7xvoqDKfbi3

ACKNOWLEDGMENTS

Many incredible people have helped me share my stories with the world. I call them my "VIPs." Book club managers and marketing agents worldwide have reached out to me about my work and want to share it with their audiences. Do you know how exciting it is to have someone eager to read your work? I can't even convince my own teenage kids to read my books! So, in this section, I want to acknowledge how important all of you are to me. I want to start with the excellent Donna B. This message is just for you: ***May the Force be with you, because you can't write a saga without a fellow Jedi! A special thank you to the "Winning Wave Alliance" of Padawans—the Jedi Council of Literature—led by the wise Jedi Mistress Donna. Your story-loving, perceptive, and all-knowing guild has been a tremendous support on my intergalactic writer's journey! So, thank you, young Jedis!***

Jedi Mistress—Sonia D. Hebdon

I want to acknowledge several outstanding individuals who have supported my writing journey. Allison Baker, Marketing Manager at Jenkins Group, has been a guiding light during the challenges of book marketing. I appreciate her positive feedback on my work and her encouragement on days when I was tempted to give up. A heartfelt thank you to my British friend, Emily Carter, and her partner, Abdulsalam Adelani, whose support for my authoring endeavors has helped me focus on autism and DID awareness through my work. Other remarkable people include James Wilson, whose kindness and shared faith have been a source of inspiration, and Cynthia Owen, who has been a lifeline to a new writer.

I want to thank Cindy Ballard, Stina Claire, ColleenWilliam, Jessamine Abraham, Solomon Carson from The Social Book Club, Steve Morton from Literary Circle Book Club, Andy Strike from Books & Banter Book Club, Alessa O. from *Books with a Sci-Fi Twist*, and *Flash Readers* for encouraging their readers to discover my stories. I also wish to extend special gratitude to an incredible '80s expert, Paul Johnson of *1980s Rewind*, and to Angie Burns of Marlow FM. Thank you for your enthusiasm for *Sincerely Yours* and the music associated with the book. Paul's extensive knowledge of '80s music promises many engaging conversations ahead. Lastly, I appreciate *Flashback_Rewind* for their kind responses regarding my role as a mother and for sharing my posts on their platform.

Chapter One

<u>A VIEW TO A KILL</u>

1968, Haven Cove

Eleanor sprinted along the jagged cliff face, lungs burning; wind ripping at her hair like invisible fingers. Panic flooded her chest. Her world felt as if it was crumbling with each frantic step. She glanced over her shoulder, her heart pounding; dread filling her eyes. How close was her pursuer? Her foot snagged on a hidden root beneath the tall grass. She stumbled and hit the ground hard; her breath was knocked out of her. Before she could rise, a shadowy figure loomed over her.

"You can't run, Eleanor!" Alaric yelled, his voice cold and low, cutting through the crashing waves below. Fear flashed across her face as she looked up at him. "I won't do it, ALARIC!" she shouted, her voice trembling with defiance. He took a step closer, his dark coat billowing in the wind. "You know you must finish the story, Eleanor, exactly as

I instructed." She pushed herself up, trembling but determined. "Where did you hide the manuscript?" he demanded, eyes narrowing. "You'll never find it," she spat, "and the story isn't finished without the last page." Alaric's jaw clenched. "The Whitlock Society won't be pleased. Without my ending, their requests go unanswered."

"I don't care!" she growled. "I won't let you twist it. I won't let you win." A flash of rage flared in Alaric's eyes. "Then we'll find another gifted writer to take your place." With a quick flick of his wrist, an unseen force shoved Eleanor backward. The wind swallowed her scream as she tumbled off the cliff into the churning sea below. The icy water closed over her as if sealing her in a frozen tomb. She struggled to reach the surface, but the current pulled her back down into the murky depths. Her lungs burned. Darkness flooded her vision. Then there was nothing. Alaric stood at the cliff's edge, watching with cruel satisfaction. He snapped his fingers, and a swirling black portal tore open in the air beside him. Without a word, he stepped through and vanished.

Far beneath the waves, something moved. Eleanor's spirit soared upward, caught in a whirl of light and water, her essence spiraling out of the depths. Suddenly, she burst from the ocean, hanging in the eye of a bright funnel of light. In a flash, she was gone, and in the quiet of Clifftop Manor, a forgotten typewriter rattled violently. Golden light spilled from its keys as an otherworldly scream tore through the room. Then, there was silence.

Eleanor's thoughts drifted back to that crucial moment when everything changed. She was no longer in the sea or standing at the cliff's edge. Everything was white and endless, humming and alive, buzzing like a faint electric current through her bones. With a jolt, she gasped and sat up.

She looked around and sat up in bed. Rubbing her eyes, she admired the Art Deco furnishings in her room as angelic light streamed through her window. She sighed in relief, feeling safe in the familiar Realm of Light where she is a Light Keeper—the Chief Editor at the Library of Dreams. She has the important task of ensuring that certain special fictional stories written on Earth are stored safely in the library. The books need to be cataloged and shelved, but the manuscripts in the repository are 'alive'—the characters in their alternate worlds live out their stories forever. When their authors die suddenly, leaving manuscripts unfinished, both the authors and the fictional characters they created become trapped in limbo until a Whitlock Writer completes the stories and releases them—the authors, the manuscripts, and their living characters—into the Realm of Light.

Eleanor jumped out of bed and looked out her window to admire the beautiful, heavenly place she now called home. Bright colors decorated her view down the hill from her room. In the distance, the large library where she worked was visible, surrounded by apple blossoms. It was paradise, with birds softly dancing in the air. She could see the workers—all dressed in white—heading to their daily jobs: the Realm of Light being much like an earthly city, only perfect; a heavenly domain created for and inhabited by deceased storywriters from the beginning of time, living and working there in peace and harmony.

On her walk to work, Eleanor saw William Shakespeare, who usually graced the town square, encouraging townspeople to listen to his plays. Eleanor often saw famous writers gather at **The Cloud & Quill Café** to discuss their work.

Prominent authors spent many hours there, often creating new works that would never reach a worldly audience but remain in their realm. The café was nestled among a grove of golden-leaved trees that shimmered like the first light of dawn. The air smelled faintly of honey and warm paper, and a gentle breeze carried the soft rustle of pages turning somewhere far away, as if heaven itself was reading.

At a corner table, three literary giants sipped steaming porcelain cups. F. Scott Fitzgerald sat pristine in a cream linen suit; his hair perfectly parted, with a faint glow of eternity smoothing every hint of past exhaustion. His eyes still held that restless, romantic gleam as he swirled the froth into his cappuccino. "You know," he said, voice coated with jazz-age charm, "Gatsby would have loved this place. All that light, all that ... unreachable beauty, except here you can reach it."

Across from him, Ernest Hemingway leaned back in his chair; shirt sleeves rolled up, arms tanned from some celestial fishing trip. His face was weathered but calm, his eyes sharp and sea grey. He took a sip of his black coffee, no sugar, and grunted, "Too pretty for me. I like a café where the coffee bites back. But this is good. Strong." He nodded toward the angels outside the window, flying past lazily, like gulls hovering over a beach, "Makes a man want to write again."

Beside them, James Matthew Barrie appeared smaller; neat in his tweed jacket, his boyish face glowing softly in the golden light spilling through the café's arched windows. His eyes sparkled mischievously as he traced circles in the air, causing tiny motes of stardust to form the outline of a pirate ship. "This is exactly the kind of place Peter would never want to leave," Barrie mused. "Though of course, in heaven, you never have to grow up unless you want to."

Around them, the cafe's marble floor seemed to hum softly, each note blending with an unseen orchestra. Outside, the River of Light slowly wound toward the distant horizon, where a perpetual sunrise lingered low in the sky. Above, the faint clatter of typewriter keys mixed with the laughter of unseen muses. The three men raised their cups in a silent toast—one to beauty, one to truth, and one to never-ending stories.

The Library of Dreams rose like a cathedral of shimmering light; its spires formed from beams of gold that sparkled in the rays of eternal dawn. Its walls were made of living crystal, each surface glittering with words that moved and danced like fireflies, telling stories to passersby. Shelves stretched endlessly upward into skies painted in soft shades of silver and pink, where angels glided silently, carrying scrolls that trailed ribbons of starlight.

The air was filled with the scent of blooming lilies and fresh parchment; a fragrant aroma that seemed to awaken the soul's deepest longing for truth. Sunbeams, warm yet gentle, streamed through windows made of translucent pearl, illuminating books bound in unknown materials, covers woven from rainbow light, and pages that whispered with the voices of their authors, each word glowing softly as if lit from within.

In the center, a large round table made of polished jasper is surrounded by chairs crafted from olive wood, cushioned for the reader's comfort. The floor beneath is a mosaic of gemstones illustrating the history of creation, subtly shifting to display new scenes as time itself is shown in greater splendor.

Books, scrolls, and letters are alive, not just with knowledge but with the very heartbeat of God's truth. When a reader opens a volume, the words rise like a warm breeze, wrapping around them in visions, allowing them to step into the story and walk beside its characters. There, nothing is lost; no tale forgotten; no wisdom misplaced. It is a place where eternity itself leans in to read.

As Eleanor entered the Library of Dreams, she immediately found herself surrounded by countless shelves filled with completed manuscripts by earthly writers, neatly arranged. She looked up at the domed ceiling, which features a stunning reproduction of Michelangelo's *Creation of Man,* as painted in the Sistine Chapel.

Eleanor approached the main circulation desk, where various authors had casually gathered to browse books and brainstorm new stories. Such stories could come to life if a talented intermediary on Earth received a message from a renowned author asking them to write in their name. However, this was rare because most humans were closed off to this kind of creativity. Eleanor then headed downstairs to the library's secluded archive, where she worked editing and shelving those special manuscripts in the deep-storage repository. Here, the characters within the original writings lived out their stories, unaware that they and their worlds are 'merely' fabrications of their authors' imaginations. These manuscripts were not accessible to the public, thus preserving the integrity of their fictional worlds. Copies of the manuscripts were made available for circulation upstairs in the main library.

Eleanor's office overlooked a stunning flower garden filled with lavender and roses. She sat at her desk, prepared to begin her daily tasks, when a sharp pain struck her chest. It felt like a glass shard had punctured her heart. She gasped for breath, softly whispering "Alaric" as her blonde hair and piercing blue eyes turned toward the portal beside her: an oval vintage mirror capable of transporting her to Earth, where she could briefly walk in the physical world. All Eleanor knew was that Alaric had found another way to complete his dark story, and if he succeeded, he would become human and cause chaos on Earth. She was now immortal: a divine, good, and pure counterpart to Alaric, the Chief Editor in the Realm of Darkness.

If Alaric gained human status, chaos would erupt on Earth, and the safety of all the deceased authors and their works in the Realm of Light would be at risk. Eleanor reflected on how, although Alaric killed her, she now possessed the power as a Light Keeper and Chief Editor at the Library of Dreams to protect the gifted earthly Conduits—the Whitlock Writers—and prevent the Realm of Light from collapsing. Sensing that Josie and Blaine were in danger, she hurried to the portal. Gently passing her hand over the mirror, a vortex with cascading white light opened, and she stepped through and vanished.

Chapter Two

<u>IT'S THE END OF THE WORLD!</u>

1990, Los Angeles

Josie stood at the edge of the cliff, stumbling as she tried to climb over the rocks. Her heart pounded as she heard Alaric behind her, screaming, "Josie, you can't get away from me this time!" She rose to her bare feet, now cut by thick blades of grass and jagged rocks. She pulled up her flowing white linen dress as she headed for safety. Alaric was only a few meters away, smiling and exposing his jagged teeth. "Run, little lamb, RUN!" he bellowed as his eyes blackened, and his presence summoned lightning to strike the ocean twice.

"The new writer, of course, is doing very well because he has a heart full of despair," Alaric said with a beaming smile. "But we destroyed the typewriter!" screamed Josie. "No, Josie, you're mistaken. You can never destroy a Whitlock Society typewriter; it's enchanted and will always repair itself," laughed Alaric.

He stepped closer, leaning down as Josie began to slip. She grabbed a large tree root but lost her footing, left hanging over the raging sea, now in full panic. "What are you trying to say?!" she screeched. Alaric bent close to her face as she dangled over the edge, feeling herself slipping as her grip started to loosen. He whispered, "I mean, you are expendable. I have someone who WILL finish my story! Goodbye, Josie Worthington!" He pushed her hands; she lost her hold and fell screaming into the deep, raging sea.

Josie woke up in a cold sweat, trembling and breathless; she barely reacted when someone in the room spoke to her, "He's back, Josie, and more powerful than ever." Josie quickly turned on her lamp to see Eleanor sitting in a rocking chair in her room. Eleanor, an angelic vision of beauty with long, flowing golden hair cascading over her shoulders, was wearing a black-and-white pantsuit. She stood and approached Josie, who was still watching in stunned amazement, Eleanor's blue eyes soft with compassion. "Eleanor," Josie inquired, now clumsily rubbing her eyes, "What are you doing here?"

"Sorry to wake you, Josie," Eleanor said, relishing the feeling of flesh, blood, and bone as she carefully crossed Josie's small college dorm to sit beside her on the bed. "You dreamed about Alaric, didn't you?" "How do you know that?" Josie asked, surprised by Eleanor's insight. "I received a message from Alaric. I felt a sharp pain in my chest, and I knew I needed to see you, so I found you dreaming about him," said Eleanor urgently, like a protective mother. Josie wrapped her blanket around herself and adjusted the pillows under her head.

"Yes, I was on a cliff top, and he was tormenting me as I tried to hold onto a twisted branch," Josie said with despair. "A branch as you dangled over the ocean?!" Eleanor's face showed distress. "Yes," Josie gasped, "Why do you ask?" "Josie, you relived how I died! I'm so sorry... Josie?! He's warning you... that the new Conduit has been chosen for the Realm of Darkness." "WHAT?" Josie exclaimed, shaking her head in disbelief. "What did Alaric say to you in your dream?" Eleanor cautiously probed, sensing how traumatic experiencing her death was for Josie. Josie responded, "He said he had the upper hand,

and the new writer was working out well for him."
Eleanor stood up, "What else did he say?"
"I questioned him, saying the typewriter was destroyed. But he said it could never be destroyed!" Josie felt vulnerable as she adjusted her blankets. Eleanor nodded slowly, "That is true, Josie. The Whitlock typewriters rebuild themselves over time, no matter what happens to them." Josie's anger grew. "Well, we're in trouble, aren't we?"
"No, Josie, that's not true!" Eleanor assured her. "What do you mean, Eleanor?" Josie pressed. "I mean, there's only one way. It's not easy, but the typewriter can be destroyed for good, and so can Alaric," Eleanor said softly. "We'll discuss this later, but first we need to find out who he has chosen," she added with calm authority.

"That sounds like finding a needle in a haystack!" Josie said dismissively. "Josie, I think Alaric has met someone here in Los Angeles," Eleanor guessed, with concern. "How do you know that?" Josie asked. "I know because the new Conduit must be chosen from a place near the old one. You weren't planning to stay in Haven Cove but wanted to move to Los Angeles. Alaric knew all that, which is why he would have picked someone here in LA." Josie shook her head. "But still, Eleanor, Los Angeles is bigger than you think."

"Josie, I think he might be someone you already know from college or from where you spend a lot of time," Eleanor responded.

"Really?" Josie asked, quizzically.

"Really!" Eleanor asserted, "Just follow your gut, stay alert, and be aware that the person chosen will make him or herself known to you."

The sounds of Josie's dorm mates stirring could be heard outside her door as they shuffled off to their morning routines. "I must go, Josie," Eleanor said as she moved toward Josie's mirror hanging above her dressing table. "Remember, Josie," she added, "You're not alone. I'll be watching and guiding you. If you need to contact me directly, go to any mirror and gently call my name." Eleanor then placed her hand on the mirror, and a golden arc of light radiated within the portal. Before disappearing, she said, "Josie, you are in control of this story, not Alaric ... Goodbye, Josie Worthington," she added, pressing her left palm softly against the mirror. A beam of white light filled the entire bedroom as she suddenly vanished. Josie sat on her bed, stunned, digesting all the information Eleanor had given her. She looked at her clock radio; it was around 8 a.m. She needed to hurry, or she'd be late for her Literary Studies lecture, which started in an hour. She jumped out of bed, quickly straightened the sheets and cover, and walked over to her stereo, pressing the Play button on the cassette deck, and REM's **"It's the End of the World"** instantly blared out of the speakers, making her smile. It's so true that no matter what you're feeling, a song can instantly match or transform your mood. Josie grabbed her clothes for the day, her towel, and toiletries, and headed to the communal bathroom just two doors from her room.

Chapter Three

<u>TELL ME WHY, I DON'T LIKE MONDAYS</u>

On Monday morning, Anthony Temple headed into town, soaking in the city life around him. Cars lined up at intersections; impeccably dressed women stilettoing their way to work; cyclists daringly weaving through traffic. He loved being able to blend in and stay unnoticed. With a Walkman strapped to his belt, he was wired for sound and listened to Wang Chung's **"Dance Hall Days."** He loved music, especially from the early '80s, and was a big fan of Wang Chung, but after a busy weekend spent writing, he found it hard to get going; Monday mornings were especially tough for him.

Loneliness is like a disease; once you catch it, it's hard to shake off. Anthony was accustomed to being alone. He's a twenty-one-year-old Honors student at the University of Southern California's Annenberg School for Journalism and Literary

Studies — a tall, sandy-blonde-haired man, gaunt but with a healthy, tanned complexion.

From a young age, he knew he was different. When he was ten, he discovered he was adopted, but his parents reassured him of their love and encouraged him not to search for his birth parents—a policy he increasingly accepted as he reasoned it was pointless to look for parents who didn't want him. That seemed crazy. As he grew older, he lurches from one obsessive hobby to another, investing heavily in each fixation. He enjoyed taking things apart to see how they worked and trusted too easily; he usually spoke with unfiltered candor. But Anthony had a talent for the written word and a remarkable gift for creative writing, so he dreamed of becoming the next Stephen King.

Anthony faced bullying from a young age. He was often teased by his peers while riding his bike to school or around his neighborhood. As the target of many practical jokes in middle school, he felt like a misfit who didn't belong anywhere. Many afternoons, he sat in his attic bedroom, staring out the window at kids playing football. He longed to be part of a group rather than someone whispered about and teased. He wanted to be seen and heard.

Writing was his lifeline; he spent hours on his mother's electric typewriter, creating fantasy and horror stories in which he vicariously became the hero, slaying dragons and rescuing damsels in distress. He longed to be in love but could barely talk to a girl without stuttering. As he grew older, he became interested in Stephen King's stories, and he wrote short stories where the kids who bullied him received their comeuppance and were put in their place. He dreamed of becoming a professional author and studied hard at school to earn good grades; his studiousness redoubling the ire of his tormentors. Although he was also the editor of the school yearbook, he would have to use that power carefully, lest it become another reason for his detractors to harass him.

Recognizing his hidden literary talent, Anthony understood it was his duty to forge his own path in life: his future was in his hands, and he couldn't blame anyone else if he failed. College was his first major step toward independence, and leaving behind those mean kids who had made his childhood miserable helped build his confidence. It was shocking for him to learn that his supposed best friend from childhood was a treacherous imposter. He had long envied Anthony because he was an A+ student and praised by teachers for his writing skills.

When Anthony was accepted to USC, moving from a small Texas town in Wharton County to the big city was initially difficult. He appreciated the anonymity on the streets of LA; it freed him from the bullying anxiety he used to experience when he was teased or mocked back home. During one of his exploratory walks, he passed a thrift store and saw an old-fashioned typewriter in the window. It looked scratched and worn, but he knew he had to have it. Anthony loved old typewriters and often imagined himself in a baroque room warmed by a large, open fireplace, smoking a pipe, typing his next bestseller at an ornate desk, sipping red wine, while a string quartet played Mozart—faithfully reproduced on his HiFi stereo.

He suddenly stopped and noticed that the shop had just opened. He had walked this way at least twice a week, and the last time the shop was empty. He gently turned the doorknob, and the doorbell chimed as he entered. Immediately, he was surrounded by unusual artifacts and was captivated by a section of taxidermized animals—fascinating and repulsive all at once. A collection of first-edition Gothic horror novels also caught his eye. He felt like he was in heaven. *What a fantastic place!* He thought excitedly.

As he slowly turned to admire the store's Deco charm, an older man with slicked-back hair behind the counter grinned with a bright yet mysterious smile. Anthony approached, feeling a bit nervous. "Hi, I'm interested in the typewriter you have in the shop window." The man's rugged jawline and dark brown eyes looked at Anthony uncomfortably, as if he was peering straight into his soul.

"Ah, yes ... the typewriter; what a find that was!" he said as he stepped out from behind the counter and faced Anthony. "Would you like to examine it?" he asked with a peculiar accent.
"Oh yes!" Anthony responded enthusiastically as the older man, with his thin, bony hands, reached into the display and carefully picked up the typewriter, carrying it back to the counter as if it were a precious newborn baby.

Anthony followed and immediately began examining the typewriter. The keys were stiff from age, and as his fingers brushed over them lightly, something stirred inside him—soft as a whisper, sharp as a memory. The ribbon was dry, as expected for a device over 30 years old. The shopkeeper plugged it in, and Anthony turned it on, hearing a gentle hum from the machine. He looked at the clerk behind the counter, who wore a grin that was far too broad to be trustworthy. "Do you think it works?" he asked, curiosity widening his eyes.

The shopkeeper leaned forward, his bright, unsettling smile resembling the Cheshire Cat's from Alice in Wonderland. "Oh, it'll write, alright!" he assured Anthony with a slow, deep voice. "Just be careful what you feed it, though," he chuckled. "I'll even throw in a new ribbon, which is rare and comes from Italy, for free. How does that sound to you?" the mysterious salesman said with a gleam in his eye, as his smile revealed gold caps. Anthony responded without hesitation— "I'll take it!"

"Good, good!" Alaric nodded, sliding the typewriter into a worn leather case. "I have a feeling you two will get along... splendidly," he hinted as he handed Anthony the machine, now safely cocooned in its leather satchel. As Anthony opened the door to leave, the strange man called out belatedly, "Young man... just out of curiosity, what genre do you write in?" Anthony stopped and turned around. "Horror!" he responded succinctly, then elaborated, "I love to write horror stories. I'm a big Stephen King fan. Is that a problem?" Anthony asked, curious why this seemed so important to the old fool. "No, that's wonderful. I sensed you were a lover of horror and things that go bump in the night," he said with a knowing grin. "Have a lovely afternoon, young man," the storekeeper bade Anthony, who quickly exited, jingling the bell above the door.

Anthony held his newly acquired, prized possession tightly as he walked through the busy streets of LA back to his dorm, eager to use his antiquated typewriter for the first time. He was only about two blocks from campus, but as he headed home, he was puzzled yet certain he could hear a faint sound coming from inside the brown leather bag that held the typewriter. Anthony shrugged it off, telling himself it was just his imagination.

He briefly glanced at his watch while keeping a steady pace and realized he didn't have much time because he needed to attend a lecture and would be locked out if he was late. Still, he planned to drop off the typewriter in his dorm room before heading straight to his class. He ran up the stairs to his room, and as he opened the door, he sensed an unusual sense of dread he'd never felt there before. He dismissed it as nerves; due to the upcoming review he was giving on *Great 20th Century Authors* in his Literature tutorial that afternoon.

He carefully placed his latest purchase on a small coffee table and took it out of its brown leather satchel. Anthony hesitated briefly, then looked at the typewriter, appreciating its age and beauty, before pressing the keys to test their response. "After class, you and I will take a test drive, my beautiful one," he said aloud. He grabbed his house keys, hurriedly slipped them into his pocket, and stepped outside into the cool early afternoon air, locking the door behind him. Inside, the room was silent except for the faint hum of the old typewriter. Suddenly, a soft, ghostly glow spilled from the device, illuminating the room and casting pale white shadows. The typewriter's keys started to move on their own, typing faded, ghostly words through the ribbon onto the loaded paper on the platen. CHAPTER ONE: New Conduit Chosen!

Chapter Four

<u>HEAD OVER HEELS</u>

Josie hurried into the lecture hall, catching her breath. The lecture had already begun, and she quickly took out her notes for the Literature class, placing her bag on the chair next to her. She was planning a late-night dinner at Blaine's parents' house after the lecture and tutorial. He would be waiting outside after the tutorial, ready to pick her up.

She was busy scribbling when she heard, "Excuse me, do you mind if I sit here?" Turning to see a tall, spindly young man with short, sandy blonde hair smiling at her, she responded encouragingly, "Of course! I don't mind at all," as she gathered her bag and placed it on the floor under her chair. He adjusted his glasses and busily pulled out his notebook. "Thanks," he said politely. "I'm Anthony." Josie smiled and shook his extended hand. "Hi, I'm Josie."

"Wow!" Anthony exclaimed in admiration as he noticed the names of various bands Josie had scrawled on the cover of her note-taking folder. "You have great taste in music," he added, gesturing toward the cover that features the Dead Kennedys, Joy Division, The Cure, and The Smiths. Josie turned and gave Anthony her full attention. "Thank you, it's nice to meet someone who appreciates good music," she said, smiling shyly. Anthony's heart skipped a beat as he looked at Josie with admiration.

"Well, it is a rare thing ..." Anthony started, but Josie gently stopped him with a whisper. "We'll talk later," she said, refocusing her attention on the lecturer. Anthony felt a little embarrassed. "Oh, sorry." Josie smiled kindly in response. "No problem."

Anthony watched this stunning girl: she seemed about nineteen or twenty, with long, straight black hair flowing past her shoulders, streaked with fiery red at the front and sides. She wore lace-up cherry-red boots, a long black lace skirt, a tight velvet corset, and a purple blood-red lace pirate shirt tied at the side. She was a sight of beauty. Why weren't there girls like this back home at Peach Creek?

Anthony wondered, then tried to focus on the presentation, but Josie stayed a distracting thought. When the lecture ended, Anthony quickly stood up, eager to be among the first to leave. Josie noticed, "Going already?" she asked, smiling. Anthony's face turned bright red. "Yes, I'm giving a presentation on HP Lovecraft at the tutorial."
"Oh? Professor Sanderson's tutorial?"
"Yes," he replied shyly, shuffling his belongings into his backpack. "I'll catch up with you another time," he added awkwardly as he adjusted his glasses.

Before Josie could say anything else, he hurried out of the lecture hall. She gently nodded, packed her things, and headed down the corridor to her next tutorial. She pushed open the door, took a seat to the side, and waited as Anthony prepared at the podium to give his tutorial. Josie pulled out her stationery and got ready, eager for class to start. Professor Sanderson entered the tutorial room with a big smile on his face. "Hello, hello, my people!" he warmly greeted the students in a friendly, almost familial manner, fitting for a young academic. As the teacher set his briefcase down, the students observed him: their hip, young professor in his early thirties, with shoulder-length hair tied back into a ponytail. He wore inexpensive sneakers, a Clash T-shirt, and black jeans. Josie knew some of the other girls in her class had crushes on the young professor. She leaned back and listened to his introduction to HP Lovecraft before passing the class over to Anthony.

Anthony was nervous at first, but he gained confidence from knowing he was finally with other young people who loved classic literature as much as he did. As he opened his presentation by describing HP Lovecraft's literary achievements, he glanced at the students gathered before him and, upon instantly recognizing the beautiful girl from the previous lecture, he froze for a moment, unable to speak. Noticing his awkwardness, Josie realized that seeing her somehow caused Anthony to lose focus, so she quickly gave him a thumbs-up to encourage him. Anthony smiled, took a deep breath, and pressed on. After finishing his presentation and receiving an appreciative round of applause, Anthony hurried back to his seat as the class emptied out. Josie quickly gathered her books, eager to see Blaine, who she knew was waiting outside, but first, she wanted to congratulate

Anthony.

A group of students gathered around Anthony to discuss his presentation, and Josie joined them, waiting for a chance to congratulate him. "Thanks," he said nervously. "I'm a big fan of H.P. Lovecraft, so I was in my element," she said with a smile. They left the tutorial room together with Professor Sanderson, who locked the room, and they followed him as he headed toward the building's glass entrance doors.

As they moved behind the professor, Anthony and Josie hurriedly discussed their main points of commonality—'80s bands and growing up in small country towns. Through the glass doors, Josie saw Blaine outside, standing next to his orange beast, his chestnut-brown hair tied in a bun, and wearing his signature leather jacket. "Oh, Anthony, I must go. I'm having dinner with my boyfriend's parents this evening," Josie said as they walked down the stairs outside, heading toward Blaine's car.

Anthony stammered nervously, "Tha, tha, that's fine, Josie. See you next week in class, then." Josie gave him a quick hug, then ran down the remaining steps, threw her bag into the car, and threw herself into Blaine's arms as he twirled her around. She giggled and kissed him passionately.

Anthony felt a sharp pang of envy in his chest as the two lovers jumped into his car and sped off into the sunset, like a scene from a Hollywood teen romance movie, while Anthony walked alone to his car. He tossed his belongings onto the backseat, and no sooner did he turn the key in the ignition than **"Head Over Heels"** by The Go-Go's roared to life on his stereo.

Anthony rolled his eyes and let the song play as he drove through the empty parking lot and onto the main road, his thoughts shifting to more urgent matters. He'd be home soon and could focus entirely on his new prized possession. He might be alone, without any friends—let alone a girlfriend like Josie—but at least he'd have a new writing tool to create a world where he was accepted and loved as a hero, rather than a shy, disheveled bookworm. At last, Anthony Temple again had control of his destiny; he could shape his world the way he wanted by simply typing his story, his journey. He softly said to himself, "I will no longer be who I was when my work is finally published."

He daydreamed on his drive home, imagining how girls would notice him once he became a New York Times bestselling author. Then *he* would be the one rejecting *them,* he thought to himself. He pulled up to his college dorm and climbed the stairs past students busily talking about this weekend's upcoming parties and accidentally bumped into a jock. "Sorry," he said politely. "Watch it, geek!" the steroid-jacked gym-junkie threatened gruffly as he continued down the stairs while Anthony scampered to his room, where he shut the door quickly behind him and locked it, his anxiety heightened by the stairway altercation.

He tossed his keys into a drawer and headed toward the typewriter on the coffee table, but he was interrupted when his TV suddenly turned on by itself. Startled, he looked around, trying to figure out how it could have powered on. He was alone in his one-bedroom dorm, or so it seemed. Then he realized that his neighbor's remote might be interfering with his TV. He turned off the TV and sat down on the couch, gazing at the typewriter in front of him and marveling at how beautiful the machine was. He ran his fingers over the keys and was surprised to see the words typed onto the otherwise blank page on the platen.

CHAPTER ONE: New Conduit Chosen!

Anthony sat back, confused. He was sure the paper was blank. *Then how? Okay, I must not have seen the page the elderly man typed to show me that the machine worked. He did type something, didn't he?* Anthony breathed a sigh of relief as he walked to his bedroom to get a new ream of paper. As he rifled through his desk drawer, he heard something... a noise behind him. Startled, he looked around, and his face paled as he realized it was the typewriter. He slowly walked to the machine where he saw another typed message on the page:

Anthony is the next horror writer extraordinaire!

His heart pounded as he struggled to comprehend what was happening. Suddenly, his radio turned on by itself. He shivered as he moved closer. There was static at first, then the radio's dial started spinning as if searching for stations. More static; then a male voice, dark and sinister…

Congratulations, Anthony. Out of a sea of a thousand dreams and countless hopefuls, you have been named the horror writer of the century. I am the merchant behind the counter of the shop where you found that old typewriter, waiting to be uncovered like buried treasure. Maybe your hands trembled as you pressed the keys? Don't worry, I don't mean to hurt you, only to carve new shadows into your stories. All I ask is that you craft a story for me when the night feels just right—a tale to echo through the darkness. Spend the coming days getting to know your new, mysterious companion. I'll be waiting in the wings, unseen but always watching.

The radio turned off just as suddenly as it had turned on, and everything went silent. Anthony stood in awe—mouth open—both amazed and frightened. At first, he thought he was hallucinating, but then the typewriter began typing. He hurried over to see what it had typed.

CARPE DIEM

He shouted aloud, translating the well-known Latin phrase: "SEIZE THE DAY!"

Chapter Five

<u>IF YOU WERE HERE!</u>

Josie sank back into the passenger seat as Blaine drove out of the university parking lot. He pressed play on his stereo, and **"Heart Break Beat"** by the Psychedelic Furs started playing. The thought that this music is the soundtrack of their relationship crossed his mind. After meeting in Haven Cove and falling in love while rescuing Eleanor and June from Alaric's dark clutches, Blaine had become an essential part of Josie's life. A year into their relationship, they moved to Los Angeles after graduating to be closer to his father, who was once the vocalist in a successful New Wave band in the late seventies but was now battling lung cancer from years of smoking.

Blaine had grown out his hair; it was no longer bleached blonde, short, and spiky, but long, chestnut brown, and shoulder-length. He often tied it in a ponytail, but he still wore his iconic black leather jacket, today over his favorite Smiths T-shirt. Though he kept his focus on the road, Josie could tell he was genuinely interested in her life and her journalism studies at USC. Blaine, a talented artist, was pursuing a fine arts degree at UCLA's School of the Arts and Architecture in Los Angeles.

He had just finished a project for his upcoming art exhibition, scheduled in a few weeks, and he smelled of turpentine and oil paints. Josie noticed splotches of red and blue paint staining his hands as he drove them to his Hollywood home. "So, do you want to tell me about your new friend?" Blaine asked inquisitively. Josie was looking out the window, a bit distracted. She hadn't had a chance to tell him about the nightmare and Eleanor's visit from the Realm of Light. If she did, she knew he would keep her hidden away like a princess in a medieval tower, guarded by a fiery dragon. "Josie?" Blaine prodded. "Oh, sorry, Blaine," she replied, realizing she hadn't been paying attention, and turned to face Blaine directly.

"His name is Anthony Temple; he's in my 20th Century Authors class," she said. Blaine pushed a little harder. "So, what's his story?" he asked, with a hint of jealousy. "He's a writer from a small town—obsessed with the horror genre—and wants to be the next Stephen King," she said, waiting for the next question. "Okay, and ..." he pressed Josie, who smiled. "Somebody's jealous ..." she playfully teased Blaine, who dropped the pretense. "Of course I'm jealous!" he responded. "Anthony gets to spend more time with you than I do!" Josie rolled her eyes and reached out her hand to Blaine. "Well, he's actually only in one tutorial class with me, and he doesn't have my heart as you do," she said with a comforting smile. "Good answer!" he snapped.

Trying to change the subject, Josie asked, "How's your dad?" Blaine shifted his gaze back to the road. "He had a bad night last night, according to mom," he explained, adding, "He had a high fever and was very weak, but he seemed better this morning." "That's good, he's doing better," Josie said with empathy, knowing the doctors told Blaine and his mother that his father only had six months to live. Even though he underwent a round of chemo and the tumor shrank, the cancer had already spread throughout his body. "He's looking forward to seeing you," Blaine said.

"I really like your father, even though he was a fool at times in the past," said Josie. Blaine smiled. "I can think of some other words to describe him," he snidely suggested. Josie smiled as they pulled into the mouth of the driveway leading to his father's impressive estate, guarded by security and surrounded by a high, gated fence. Blaine drove slowly through the open wrought-iron gates, each bar glinting like it was shooting tiny bolts of lightning beneath the floodlights at the entrance.

He paused at the security checkpoint. A plump, balding man in uniform leaned forward with a broad, friendly smile. "Hey there, Blaine, is your masterpiece finished yet?" Blaine flashed a cheeky grin. "Not yet, but soon, Harry; real soon."

"Hi, Josie!" Harry greeted her warmly as he wiped his forehead with a handkerchief. "It's hot tonight." Blaine smiled, "Sure is, Harry. I'll catch you later. Give my love to Cheryl." Harry grinned widely. "I sure will, Blaine. Bye, Josie!" "Bye, Harry." Josie politely said farewell to Harry as Blaine shifted the gear into first, and they proceeded down the driveway, which was slick and shiny like a black vinyl record, pulling them into a world where the 1980s never ended. Even the tires rolling over the small bits of gravel on the surface sounded like a stylus on an old, scratchy record, popping and crackling randomly. Palm trees lined the driveway, their trunks wrapped in tube lighting that pulsed and strobed in turns: hot pink, acid green, and electric blue.

The mansion looked like a grand, unapologetic cathedral of excess. White stucco walls shimmered under floodlights, while glass panels reflected the night lights like shards on a mirror ball. An enormous chrome guitar statue, its strings lit with tiny lights, leaned against the entrance. Windows glowed with golden light. The doors, ten feet tall and glossy-black lacquered, each with a handle shaped like a silver serpent. They promised one thing: beyond them, time stops, and rules break down as one enters the untamed heart of an '80s musician's domain.

They pulled into his father's oversized garage, parked alongside his motorcycle and some muscle cars from his collection, then headed up the stairs into the house. Blaine's mom, Grace, was busy cooking in the kitchen, while Blaine's dad, Dean, relaxed on the couch in the lounge room, wrapped in a blanket and watching a football game. The smell of homemade lasagna wafted through the house. "Is that my Josie and the Pussycats?" Dean asked rhetorically upon hearing Josie's voice. Josie walked into the lounge room. "How's my favorite rockstar?" she quipped as she bent down to give him a warm hug.

Dean's face lit up as he briefly wrapped his arms around Josie, then encouraged her and Blaine to sit down on the couch opposite him, where they made themselves comfortable. "So," he said, "What's new in the world of the next Pulitzer Prize-winning journalist, Josie Worthington?" Josie smiled cheerfully, "Not much, just settling into university life, studying, getting used to living away from home."

"Ah, the joys of youth!"

He then turned to his son and asked, "How's the latest project coming along?"

"Pretty good, Dad; it should be finished in a week."

"Good to hear you're on track, son!" he said encouragingly.

Dean Cordwell has become a shadow of his former self since battling cancer. The former lead singer of The Vibes still looks handsome, but he has grown frail. Once, he was the kind of man people envisioned when they thought of a rock legend—broad shoulders covered in leather, a jaw shadowed with stubble and rebellion, eyes blazing with the wildfire that only youth and fame can ignite. His dark, unruly hair fell across his face as he sang; sweat glistened beneath the stage lights while thousands screamed his name. Every movement was electric, every grin defiant. He lived fast, sang louder, and believed—like all rock legends do—that the music would never end. But now, the fire flickers low. The leather has been replaced with soft wool and cotton, and the stage lights with the pale glow of a television. His once-commanding frame has thinned, the angles of his bones pressing softly against his shirt. His hands, once powerful enough to bend a microphone stand, tremble as he lifts a glass of water. The tattoos that once spoke of freedom and fury are faded, their colors paling like memories whispered through smoke.

His breathing had become shallow, with each inhale a struggle and each exhale a sigh of both surrender and waning strength. Yet his eyes, though shadowed and weary, still sparkled with the essence of who he was. When he smiled faintly, it was with the grace of someone who has experienced both the heights of worldly spectacle and pleasure, and its quietest, darkest corners. There is no stage now, no audience—but the music persists—softer, slower, more fragile. You can almost hear it in his breathing rhythm, in the gentle rasp in his voice that says: *I have lived a full life*. Their moment was interrupted when Blaine's mom entered the lounge room. "Dinner's ready!" she declared with satisfaction, smiling lovingly at her husband. Blaine helped his father up and handed him his walking cane, and they slowly moved to the dining room. They sat down, and Blaine's mom prayed over the food, their visitors, and her husband's health. Since his terminal illness diagnosis, Dean had returned to his childhood faith.

He knew his time was nearly up and wanted to make amends with Blaine and Grace for his past mistakes. After asking for God's blessing on their meal, the family relaxed into a pleasant conversation, discussing Blaine's upcoming art exhibition. Josie watched the loving family dynamic, wondering if her dad would have been happy to see his young daughter all grown up. What would it be like to sit at a family meal and have her dad chatting away as if there weren't a problem in the world? What if he had survived his heart attack? What if his friends knew how to perform CPR?

These questions haunted her for years. Her mom was back in Haven Cove working night shifts as usual, but she had recently started seeing a pediatrician and was happy again. Life had become very busy, and here she was, enjoying a family dinner—those simple family pleasures that would only last a few more months before Blaine's dad would pass away. *Live in the moment,* she thought, and she could see how happy Blaine and his mom were—content for now—and that was good enough for Josie.

Later that night ...

Josie stayed in the guest room at Blaine's house because his parents upheld traditional values, which Josie and Blaine also shared. He was right next door if she needed him, and she was old-fashioned in that regard anyway, determined to wait until marriage—something Blaine admired. Blaine was downstairs in his art studio working on a new project, while Josie, exhausted, went to bed early.

She closed her eyes, and it didn't take long for her to drift into a deep sleep. She was back at Haven Cove on the cliff top where Eleanor lost her life in '68. Josie wasn't alone; a sea of unrecognizable souls surrounded her, all dressed in white, standing still, all with the same soulless eyes, staring at her. Josie looked out to sea—a storm was rapidly approaching. She was dressed in a long, flowing white gown, which made her stumble over the rocks.

"Josie!" called an unmistakably sinister voice behind her that she immediately recognized. "Alaric?!" she shouted, panicking as she spun around to face her pursuer, who she could now see was dressed in a dark trench coat—his eyes red and piercing, with teeth sharp as razors.
"What do you want, ALARIC?" Josie screamed as she frantically scrambled over the rocks, barely keeping her footing. "It's not long now!" Alaric hissed like a snake ready to strike. "What's not long now?" Josie demanded, terrified. Alaric chuckled maniacally, his demented cackle cutting through the night air. "The Whitlock Society meeting!" he grunted at last. "You did receive the invitation I left for you at the prom, did you not?"

"It was you?! You were the one who left that invitation on top of my purse!" she shot back.

"Of course, Josie, the Whitlock Society is really eager to meet you," Alaric remarked sinisterly.

"Why, Alaric? You've got a new writer; you don't need me anymore!"

"Is that what Eleanor told you?" he asked, disdain evident in his voice. "Josie, Josie ... you have a gift that the Whitlock Society needs."

Josie kept climbing over the large boulders and scraped her knees, starting to bleed right away.

"I don't want any part of this!" she boldly declared.

"But you have to attend—both you and Blaine—the invitation stated it was for two," Alaric smiled.

Just then—an almighty CRACK!—Lightning struck the raging sea below, so close there was no gap between the brightly flashing lightning and the deafening thunder. Josie immediately lost her footing and fell, grabbing an overhanging rock at the cliff's edge. Alaric moved in close and pressed the heel of his boot into her hand. She was in agony, the pain like needles piercing her fingertips. "Let go, Josie," Alaric snarled forcefully, "It's time to WAKE UP!" Josie couldn't bear the pain any longer and released her grip, screaming as she plunged toward the ocean below.

"Josie?! JOSIE!" Blaine shouted desperately as she woke up in a pool of sweat, breathing heavily and feeling dizzy from hyperventilating. She was dazed, rubbing her hands, which had red welts on the knuckles from Alaric's boots. Once she realized she was in the guest room at Blaine's house, she burst into tears. Blaine embraced Josie tightly. His long, dark hair now fell loosely in curls around his shoulders; his overalls were covered in acrylic paint. "Hey Jose ..." he said softly, "I'm here ... nothing will harm you. Relax, baby ... breathe slowly," he said in a gentle, calming voice as he held her. "A ... La ... Alaric!" she blurted out, sobbing as she buried her face in Blaine's shoulder. After a few tender moments, Blaine noticed Josie's reddened knuckles. His face flushed with anger as he stared at her hands.

"Josie?" Blaine asked knowingly.

"He's not giving up, Blaine," Josie said with resignation.

Josie jumped off the bed and started pacing around the room. "He's never going to stop, Blaine!" Josie warned as her man stood and grabbed her shoulders, trying to calm her down.

"Josie, look at me," Blaine said, calming her panic. "Josie!" he said steadily and sincerely, "I love you!" She stopped abruptly and looked into his eyes. "I ... I love you, too, Blaine!" she admitted as he leaned in and kissed her tenderly. Suddenly, the stars aligned, and everything felt right, like it was when they first kissed at the reservoir in Haven Cove. She closed her eyes and savored this fragile, wonderful moment—his gentle touch, his soft lips, and his warm breath—and the deep, heartfelt love they shared. She gently pulled back to see the smile spreading on his face, returning it with her own. "Josie," he said excitedly, "We can do anything together, you know that." Calm and confident now, she wrapped her arms around him.

"Wait," he said, stepping away to press Play on the stereo. She laughed. Music was their love language. It was The Thompson Twins' **"If You Were Here"**—quirky, slow, and exuberant—as he returned and pulled her into another embrace. Resting her head softly on his shoulder, they swayed gently to the music together.

Blaine's mother and father stood at the door, peering in after hearing Josie scream. They both smiled and dared not interrupt the moment. "He gets the smooth talk from me, you know," Dean suggested cheekily, wheezing as he spoke. "All right, Casanova," Grace responded. "Yes, it's like looking back in time when you and I first met," she added, gazing at them fondly. "Come on," he said, "let's go put on some music in our room and make our own magic," he said, slowly catching his breath. Grace blushed. "You're not well, Dean, but you still have a way with words," she said, smiling as they both gently shut the door and headed to their bedroom.

"What was that?" Josie asked Blaine, looking up. "It was mom and dad checking in on us; they must've heard you scream," Blaine answered. She tried to push him away. "Don't you dare," he whispered. "You'll ruin the moment, and anyway, they're gone."

"Oh," she said, leaning her head back on his shoulder, soaking in the feeling of being in love with the rockstar's son who stole her heart and her record collection. Josie eventually drifted off to sleep in Blaine's arms, with Eurythmics' **"Sweet Dreams"** softly playing in the background. She felt safe with Blaine. After more than a year of dating, she knew Blaine was the one she wanted to spend the rest of her life with.

As she grew tired, her earlier worries resurfaced. The summer solstice approached, and that frightened her because Blaine and she had been called to the Whitlock Society Esoteric Writers Retreat on the longest day of the year—June 21. Time was running out, and the secret society using writers to manipulate Alaric was about to be exposed and confronted. She would finally meet the puppet masters and learn what they truly wanted from her.

Blaine gently kissed her forehead. "Get some sleep, Josie. You need to stop overthinking everything." She opened her eyes and saw his beautiful face smiling at her. Over the past year, he had truly become an incredible man to her, so supportive of her writing career. His gorgeous eyes always seemed like windows into his soul, as if she could see exactly what he was thinking. His hair looked stunning. His hair is a rich, dark brown, cascading to his shoulders in soft, shimmering strands that catch the light with every movement. His once-fierce, punk-bleached haircut was replaced by a more natural, healthier style, reflecting how Blaine was finally at peace with his father—and himself.

His transformation was evident in his appearance and renewed confidence, radiating genuine happiness. With Blaine, life was simple, and now they were building their future together. He was spending as much time as possible with his father to mend their once-shattered relationship.

Blaine had created a beautiful art studio downstairs, a sanctuary from the world. He had always dreamed of being an artist, and his father was funding his first major exhibition before he passed away. So, Blaine had been busy for the past few months making artwork for the launch, which was scheduled in two weeks. Josie started drifting off to sleep, and she could sense Blaine losing energy and beginning to doze off as well. Exhausted, both fell into a deep sleep, happy to be together and in love. No matter what the Whitlock Society retreat brought them, they had this moment, and that was all that mattered.

Chapter Six

<u>I COULD BE HAPPY!</u>

Eleanor sat lost in a trance at her desk, initially unaware of her assistant's gentle knock on the door. She looked up, snapping back to reality. "Marcus?" she asked. "I'm sorry I didn't hear you there," she said, glancing at the manuscripts on her desk she'd been reading, then at the doorway through which Marcus had entered. He was a handsome man in his twenties, an Irish writer who died in a car accident in the '80s. His sandy blonde hair fell loosely around the collar of his pinstriped suit, a dapper dresser in life and in death. "Sorry for disturbing you, Ellie," he hesitated as Eleanor gestured for him to sit in the club chair in front of her desk. "What's up with you?" he surprised Eleanor, catching her off guard.

"How do you know something's wrong, Marcus?" Eleanor asked her assistant, who quickly replied, "I know you well enough to sense that something's off. It's written all over your face." She put her pen down, leaned back in her chair, stretched out her hands, then brought them back in and cracked her knuckles as she spoke. "It's Josie. Alaric contacted her through another dream." Marcus's face immediately tightened with concern. "I understand..." he said anxiously, while she smiled warmly at Marcus, who, honestly, was the kind of guy she would have dated when she was alive. Fully satisfied in every way in the Realm of Light, her passion was to ensure the safety of the characters living their fictional lives in all those stories, because if those characters were to discover their worlds aren't real, the entire Realm of Light could collapse, and chaos could ensue on Earth.

Alaric is taunting Josie in her dreams. I want to intervene, but I'm only supposed to guide her," Eleanor explained. Marcus's face tightened in thought for a moment as he joined Eleanor in analyzing the situation aloud. "What does he want? Does he have a new writer? The Whitlock Society's annual meeting is in two weeks, so we still have time to figure out what Alaric is up to," Marcus suggested. Eleanor said, "He's up to no good!" "Of course, Ellie. This is Alaric, the Chief Editor of the Realm of Darkness," Marcus added. He paused briefly before asking, "What happens if the Chief

Editor of the Realm of Light or the Realm of Darkness convinces a writer to bring them to life?" That question made Eleanor look worried, and she warned, "The realms of light and darkness would cease to exist, as would fictional story-writing," she said anxiously. "What do you mean?" Marcus asked Eleanor. "There would be no more creative magic to craft new stories; storytelling would come to an end! As a former writer..." she said sadly, "A world lacking storytelling feels tragic!" Eleanor closed the journal she had been writing in earlier. "Marcus?" Eleanor asked nervously, "Were you satisfied with how the Whitlock Conduit finished your manuscript?"

"I have never seen how it ended, Eleanor. I mean, I didn't find out until I entered the Realm of Light that my agent sent my unfinished work to the Whitlock Society. Clara, my fiancée, didn't even know I sent my agent an unfinished hard-copy manuscript," explained Marcus, tears welling in his eyes, "If only I could see how my story ended ..." "What if? ... No, we can't do that!" Eleanor paused briefly, now choosing her words more carefully. "What if you could visit that realm, see your story come to life, and witness the ending? Of course, we

must stay unseen and unknown. Do you think it would help to see how your words breathe life into the beautiful world you've built for your characters?" A warmth spread across Marcus's face. "Would you do that for me, Ellie?"
"Yes …" she hesitantly affirmed, feeling uncomfortably aware that her fondness for Marcus might be showing. "Yes, I would!" she added quickly, "... But let's think of it as a future project after we've dealt with Alaric and our realm is safe again."

"Yes, I agree, Ellie: there's plenty of time. I should check on the staff at the front desk. I know there was some trouble with Oscar Wilde this morning, demanding to see the original copy of one of his works stored in the archive, no doubt," Marcus smiled. Eleanor giggled. "Yes, that's all we need, Oscar Wilde visiting his own stories' worlds." Marcus laughed. "I'd better go, Ellie. See you at lunch?" he suggested, shyly meeting Eleanor's eyes with admiration and something more. "I'd love that, Marcus," she replied as he briefly waved and left the office. Eleanor took a deep breath. Marcus had become more than just an assistant to her, but she had only been in love once—with Thomas, a

Whitlock Society official high up in the organization. He was the last thought that crossed her mind as Alaric pushed her off the cliff to her death.

Eleanor felt silly for dwelling on the past. She was no longer chained to a Whitlock typewriter and was living an extraordinary life as a Light Keeper. Still, a longing remained in her heart for something more. Could romantic love exist in the Realm of Light as it does on Earth, among pure souls without physical bodies? All she knew was that Marcus was the only man besides Thomas who tugged at her heartstrings, and she could feel her heart race when he was near.

Marcus left Eleanor's office, lost in thought about his past as he slowly made his way back to the circulation desk upstairs. A talented Irish writer who had published a novel that won many prestigious awards, he was working on its sequel when a drunk driver ran a red light and hit his car while he was returning home from a business meeting with his agent in 1986. He died instantly, leaving his high school sweetheart and recently engaged fiancée, Clara, devastated. Their planned wedding day was only two weeks after his death.

He attended his funeral, watching family and friends comfort her. He also saw her pack his belongings to donate to Goodwill. His last incomplete manuscript sat neglected on his computer and was never revisited—so she wiped the hard drive and donated the computer to charity. His publisher contacted her about the manuscript, but Clara told her it was gone. Clara believed his final story should die with him, blaming his literary agent for Marcus's death because of her insistence on meeting him on that cold, wet September night when he crashed on his drive home. Clara sold their house and moved back to London to start fresh.

As a book marketer, she could work anywhere, and she knew that without Marcus, she had to start over somewhere else. Later, Marcus sat in the back row at Clara's wedding to a well-known London book editor, lost in 'what-if' thoughts. He was there when she gave birth to her first child, finally realizing she had moved on, and it was time he did the same. He watched Clara sleep with the newborn in the crib next to her hospital bed. He sat down to reflect on their many years together. Their first kiss was at a school dance when they were sixteen. The day he first told her he loved her was so profoundly impactful. All those memories flooded back as he slowly leaned over, gently kissed her forehead, and whispered lovingly into her ear, "You will always be my one true love, Clara," and parted forever. What Marcus never knew was that Clara, softly awakened, called out his name.

Was Eleanor his second chance at love? They shared many similarities, such as being talented writers whose careers were cut short, and they had similar tastes in music. He wished he could tell Eleanor how he truly felt about her. The thought that she might take him to the realm where his unfinished earthly manuscript had come to life— where characters live out their stories forever—was something he desperately yearned for. He longed to see how his story ended, the way it was meant to, thanks to a Conduit who finished it so his characters could exist in their own world, and his soul could be released to live in the Writers' Realm for all eternity.

A paradise created by God exists to inspire authors and motivate the next generation of writers on Earth, often without them even realizing it. That unexpected idea for a story—where do you think it comes from? The Writers' Realm is where famous writers constantly share their ideas for new stories that flow down to Earth through the ether to inspire authors. A suitably inspired writer seated at a typewriter—or nowadays, a computer—creates the story, having no idea where it came from but knowing it is better than what they could have conceived. Essentially, that is the role of the Writers' Realm: a creative sanctuary built solely to empower writers to pass their stories to future generations, germinating new tales worldwide.

Marcus knew that Josie was vital in saving this realm. If Alaric got his way, he and all the other famous writers gathered here would vanish. He couldn't let that happen, nor could he let Eleanor fail. He decided to do everything he could to help Eleanor defeat Alaric, so he could have a second chance at love. Lost in these thoughts, he took his morning break, sitting on a bench outside and soaking in the peaceful atmosphere of the writer's world. The scent of lavender, the feeling of safety in a perfect world. A song came to mind: **"I Could Be Happy"** by Altered Images. He loved hearing that song in his head while writing, and for Marcus, it was perfect—just like Eleanor. He felt happy because, for the first time since proposing to Clara, he had a sense of purpose. He was determined not to let Eleanor down, no matter what.

Chapter Seven

<u>THE MIRROR MAN</u>

It was about three in the morning when Anthony suddenly sat up in bed, a cold sweat sticking to his skin. His hand shook as he wiped his damp forehead and swung his legs over the side of the bed, feeling the rough texture of the carpet beneath his feet. He slowly made his way to the bathroom in the dark. When he flipped the switch, the light hesitated for a moment before bursting to life with a loud buzzing noise, the room dimly lit by a flickering fluorescent bulb that sputtered like a dying star. Frustrated, he gently pounded the wall, muttering, "Stupid electrics," and then fixed his gaze on the bright, cool porcelain sink, where he ran some water onto his trembling hands. He leaned in to splash his face; the icy water stung his skin. When he looked up at the cracked mirror, a sudden jolt shot down his spine as he saw something behind his reflection, staring at him with an unsettling intensity.

The bathroom light flickered ominously, casting shadows that danced across the floor. In the dim glow behind him, reflected in the mirror, he saw a tall, elderly man cloaked in a tattered black coat, with vacant eyes staring with a hollow, soulless glare. Sharp, nail-like teeth flashed as the man's cracked lips curled into a menacing smile. Heart pounding, he spun around desperately, but the tiny bathroom was eerily empty, aside from the oppressive buzzing of the fluorescent tube.

Anthony was momentarily paralyzed with fear, convincing himself that he was experiencing heat-induced hallucinations. He dabbed his sweaty face with a damp towel, avoiding his eyes in the mirror to prevent inviting more horror. He shut the bathroom door tightly with his trembling hand and slipped back into his bed, fearing the unknown dangers lurking in the shadows.

Anthony's heart pounded in his chest as his eyes darted around the shadows in fear. Every creak of the old apartment sent a jolt of panic through him, and the darkness felt alive, closing in. Surely, no one was in the shadows—it was just his mind playing tricks, he told himself—and yet an icy dread clung to him. Was there an intruder hiding in the dark?

Suddenly, a cold voice cut through the shadows, hollow and echoing: "Anthony." It was a sinister whisper that prickled his skin. Sitting calmly in his armchair was a dark, featureless silhouette wearing a hat—a living nightmare. Anthony hesitated before reaching out to turn on his bedside light, but the stern voice in the darkness stopped him cold: "No, Anthony. Keep the light off." His voice trembling, Anthony managed to rasp, "Who are you?"

The shadow shifted slightly, silently menacing, then slowly rose and straightened, remaining unnervingly still for a moment before creeping around the room, a silhouette against the darkness—an unsettling, haunting presence that seemed to emanate from some unnatural, evil place.

"My name is Alaric, Anthony," the voice crooned softly, almost mockingly. "... And I see you haven't been using the typewriter." Anthony's breath hitched as he sat up rigidly, his fingers trembling as he searched for something, anything to defend himself. "Anthony ... I'm not here to hurt you," the shadow whispered condescendingly, strangely self-assured and eerily calm. "I've come to help."

"Help?" Anthony squealed incredulously, his voice rough with suspicion. "Breaking into my apartment at 3 a.m.—that's your idea of help?!" The figure paused, Anthony sensing his unseen amusement.

Anthony, listen carefully: You've been chosen from among many writers for a special reason. And I know you're a fan of horror stories ..." A cold sweat broke out on Anthony's forehead, dread pooling in his stomach as he realized he was dealing with something much darker than he had imagined—something infernal. "Something ... inhuman?" Alaric gently teased, finishing Anthony's thoughts. "How did you know?" Anthony responded fearfully. Alaric let out a faint, disdainful chuckle that echoed softly in the dim room.

"Anthony," Alaric's eyes sparkled in the darkness, briefly lit by the pale glow of the typewriter's keys. "You have been given a great gift. This typewriter pulses with a power that exceeds your wildest dreams, a silent force ready to reshape your world." The shadowy nightmare smiled.

"My name is Alaric, and I am the Chief Editor at the Realm of Darkness," he proclaimed. Anthony whimpered, his voice threatening to break from his suffocating fear, but Alaric cut him off with a cold, metallic command. "Quiet!" he hissed, eyes gleaming with menace. "You're a horror writer, craving fame and riches from the darkness. I can give you everything you seek if you only use the typewriter that was entrusted to you." The air grew thick with an ominous chill as shadows seemed to twist and gather around.

Anthony's eyes nervously fixated on a faded, leather-bound manuscript lying beside the typewriter, whitened in the dim light. The grizzled voice hissed some instructions: "We don't have much time, Anthony. Listen ..." The specter's hand pushed the dusty tomb forward, its cracked cover whispering of secrets long buried. "All the answers are sealed within these ancient pages ..." Shadows danced around them as he leaned in closer, Alaric's voice dropping to a whisper. "Finish what was begun years ago, and you'll become the next master of horror, shaping the nightmares of your generation."

Anthony hesitated, his hand trembling as he reached out to touch the mysterious manuscript. Suddenly, Alaric's cold voice crackled, "There's an invitation waiting for you on the kitchen bench, an exclusive retreat for writers ... but beware, not all invitations are as benign as they seem." It served as a chilling reminder of the darkness behind the promise of wealth and fame.

Anthony tried to speak, but fear prevented him from forming words. "You do this for me, and the world will be your oyster, my boy," Alaric hissed, attempting to sound magnanimous, then moved to the freestanding mirror in a corner of the room. Gently touching it, a black hole opened in the mirror, releasing distant screams of terror. "Remember, Anthony, this is our little secret!" Alaric warned menacingly as he stepped into the mirror, and the portal closed behind him.

Anthony paused briefly, a mix of shock and excitement washing over him as he absorbed the chilling yet exhilarating truth. As he approached the manuscript, he thought, *I'm going to be a great horror story writer!* He clenched his fingers around the leather-bound book, its surface warm and velvety under his touch. He stroked the aged cover, feeling the cool, smooth texture of the worn leather, as each crease and scar seemed to whisper stories of the past. He carried the written tomb to his bedroom. The intricate Old English font on the cover appeared to shimmer faintly in the dim light, hauntingly beautiful and vibrantly alive as he placed it on his bedside table.

He carefully lifted the heavy cover, releasing the musty smell of dust and faded parchment that seeped into his senses like a ghostly whisper from forgotten times. Fascinated by the spectral mystery of the hidden story, he glanced at the title: *The Phantom Chronicles*. His fingers trembled slightly as he turned on the bedside lamp, instantly casting a warm glow over the yellowed pages. He read the first chapter, immersing himself in ancient words until exhaustion pulled him into sleep.

The song "Mirror Man" by The Human League suddenly and loudly blared from Anthony's radio speakers, shattering the still quiet of the morning and waking him from a deep sleep. Dazed, Anthony stretched carelessly... until a jolt of terror ran through him as Alaric's haunting visit came to mind and quickly flooded his thoughts. He nervously groped at the table in the diffused morning light, wondering if the mysterious book was real or just the remains of a bad dream. The book lay closed on the cold floor beside his bed, an ancient relic that seemed to whisper and breathe its haunting story through its very skin. Rising from his bed, Anthony moved to the kitchenette, overwhelmed but instinctively craving coffee.

 On the counter lay an envelope addressed to him. Startled, Anthony opened it and pulled out an invitation. Inside, elegantly scripted on thick ivory stationery, were a few cryptic sentences.

You enjoy things that go bump in the night?

Seize your destiny and grasp what's right in front of you!

Also in the envelope was an elegantly designed ticket, dated June 21, 1990. The ticket, addressed to Anthony Temple, was for the Whitlock Society Esoteric Writers' Retreat, to be held at Whitlock Estate in Los Angeles.

Chapter Eight

<u>FEELS LIKE HEAVEN</u>

A large banner fluttered outside the art gallery, its bright colors catching the evening light. The banner displayed Blaine's self-portrait, a striking image with bold brushstrokes, along with the caption "CORDWELL—the Artist Behind the Music!" Josie paused briefly, captivated by the lively sign as bits of street dust swirled around her feet. No time to waste; her last class had made her late for Blaine's debut art exhibition.

Glancing at her watch, she saw it was close to eight, so she was still on time, but only just. Hurriedly climbing the stone stairs and slipping on her high heels, she stepped through the grand, ornate entrance to the gallery. The space was open, filled with the smell of fresh paint and the warm glow of track lighting, illuminating various artworks hanging along satin walls.

Blaine's father's music played softly in the background as staff in matching T-shirts, decorated with prints of Blaine's self-portrait, offered hors d'oeuvres and champagne to the guests. She pushed through the crowd after spotting Blaine across the room with his parents, posing for publicity shots in front of his artwork. When she saw Josie making her way toward him through the busy room, Blaine paused and grinned. "Josie!" he said excitedly as he motioned to her. "Excuse me, Brad, but my girlfriend is here."

"Yeah, sure, Blaine. Go get her," the photographer said with a sly grin. Blaine wore sleek black leather pants that fit tightly against his legs, shimmering under the bright lights. His silver-and-black silk shirt shifted gently with every move, catching glints of light like molten metal. His signature Cherry Dr. Martens boots, scuffed and rebellious, finished his nonconformist look. His chestnut-brown hair was carefully slicked back with gel, highlighting the sharp angles of his attractive features, and gathered into a neat ponytail hanging over the back of his neck, giving him an effortlessly polished yet edgy vibe. "Hey, Josie and the Pussycats," he joked as he embraced her, twirling her around playfully. The room went silent, everyone fixed on the lovebirds in admiration, except for one young woman watching intently.

Adeline McCarther was an art student at the same college as Blaine. She had an elegant, tall, slim figure with long, golden-blonde hair intricately braided down her back. Her sleek black dress fit snugly, highlighting her curves, and she wore shiny patent-leather pumps with risqué fishnet stockings, adding a touch of rebellion. Her two friends, similarly dressed, flanked her, their laughter blending with the soft hum of conversation and the blooming lights overhead.

Karen leaned in and muttered, "Is that the girlfriend?" eyes narrowing slightly. Adeline's lips curled into a sly smile. "Yes, for now," she replied with malicious intent, breaking into insolent giggling that blended with the others in a playful echo that basked in the warm glow of the gallery. The shorter, plump girl, whose cheeks were flushed with excitement, leaned closer to Adeline. "If anyone can split them up, it's you, Addie." Her endorsement was imbued with admiration. Adeline raised her champagne flute, the crystal catching the light and sparkling as she toasted, "Cheers to that!"

she declared shamelessly, their laughter ringing above the tinkling of fine glass: the trio's mirth bubbling girlishly, reveling in their mischievous plans.

Blaine took Josie's hand and pulled her aside for a moment alone. She looked stunning in a black-and-gold cocktail dress with spiderweb edging sewn into the lace ruffle. She wore black seam stockings and pumps; her long black hair was gathered into a French bun, with loose bangs framing her face.

"You look beautiful," he complimented her sincerely. "You don't look too bad yourself," she replied in kind. "I have a surprise for you later," Blaine said with a cheeky smile. "Really?" Josie asked, surprised, pulling a strand of loose hair away from her cheeks. "Just wait and see ..." Blaine teased as some photographers caught up with them, and they paused to pose for a few shots. Josie soon felt uncomfortable with all the attention, but Blaine's parents also approached, put their arms around them, and smiled, while the paparazzi continued to flash their cameras.

When the strobing stopped, Blaine's father thanked the press and said he needed to rest. Blaine's mom pointed to a nurse approaching with a wheelchair, and Blaine's father sat down, out of breath but satisfied. He was given an oxygen mask, took a few deep breaths, and then returned the mask. Blaine's mom smiled politely, waved to their company, then turned and followed the nurse wheeling Dean to a side room to rest.

Blaine's mom was a vision of beauty; for a woman in her forties, Grace had maintained her appearance well, with gorgeous shoulder-length blonde hair and sparkling blue eyes that lit up when she smiled. Wearing a snug vinyl jumpsuit and corset, she could have been another Charlie's Angel; she looked so stunning and sassy in that outfit. She was also beautiful on the inside, volunteering for charities that helped underprivileged children. Blaine was her pride and joy! In her late forties, Dean was still a very handsome man, his long dark hair now streaked with gray. He had aged noticeably in recent months due to his cancer treatment, but the love between him and his wife remained strong. Blaine's mother knew time was running out, and she was determined to spend every waking moment with her husband—the love of her life.

Blaine's father hired a string quartet to perform a variety of modern songs while guests, the press, and the art community mingled, stopping now and then to admire Blaine's twelve new paintings. The artworks depicted different subjects, from modern landscapes inspired by photos he took during his time in Haven Cove to a large self-portrait, distorted to resemble his father's idealized image from his youth, gazing back at him in a mirror. "Excuse me, Josie ..." said the gallery director, "But I need to take the man of the hour away to meet some important people." Blaine held her arm firmly. "I'm sorry, Josie, I won't be long," he assured her as he was gently pulled away by the gallery director. "That's okay ... Go, be adored!" she joked, and as he turned to leave, he replied, "I already have the only person I want to be adored by." Josie smiled and took another sip of her champagne.

Josie enjoyed a few peaceful moments alone, but then she heard a young woman's voice behind her. "Well, don't you look lonely?" Josie turned to face a tall blonde, flanked by two other girls. Adeline. "Hi, Josie, I haven't met you, but I'm Addie. This is Karen and Bell. We go to art college with Blaine."

"Oh, hi, nice to finally meet Blaine's artist friends," Josie said, trying to balance her drink and shake the girls' hands at the same time. "So ..." Addie began, sounding like a snake, *"You're* Josie and the Pussycats—Blaine talks about you all the time!"

"Oh?" Josie responded, a flush of embarrassment washing over her, reddening her usually pale skin, "I'm sorry you have to hear that."

"No, that's alright," Bell interjected. "It's wonderful to put a face to the name, finally." Josie instinctively felt uncomfortable and looked over at Blaine, hoping to be rescued, but he was surrounded by artists and gallery owners praising his work. He looked so happy in that moment, being recognized as an artist in his own right, rather than living in the shadow of his rockstar father.

"Josie?" a familiar voice called. "There you are!" She turned to look and was surprised to see Anthony Temple approaching her, looking very debonair in a black tailcoat, with his hair teased and his big green eyes glowing warmly—Josie noticing how handsome he was without glasses. She was both stunned and relieved. She hadn't seen Anthony in weeks because he had been absent from class due to illness, but here he was, unknowingly ready to rescue her from an inquisition and looking very healthy indeed! Seeing him so sharply dressed and well-groomed was a revelation for Josie, as if she was seeing a completely different person from the goofy guy she had met in English Literature class all those months ago.

Sorry, ladies! I don't mean to interrupt, but I urgently need to talk to Josie about a journalism project we're both working on," he said charmingly yet confidently. The girls, stunned, excused themselves and scooted back under the rock from which they came. "What journalism project?" Josie asked, smiling. "The one I made up to rescue you from those piranhas," he explained, grinning confidently and clearly pleased with himself. "Well, thank you, kind sir. I owe you one," Josie replied, playfully raising her drink in admiration of Anthony's chivalry. "The pleasure is all mine," he said, graciously accepting the compliment. "I must say, the flu definitely agrees with you," Josie responded. Anthony quipped, "You look amazing!" She added rather boldly. Anthony blushed. "Why, thank you, fair maiden," he flirted in response, raising his champagne glass toward her. Josie burst into laughter. "So, what are you doing here?" Anthony couldn't tell her that Alaric, his horror writing mentor, had given him an invitation to this art exhibition, so he had to lie. "Oh, a friend of mine—her mother owns the gallery, and she gave me an invitation," he said, managing to mislead Josie without feeling particularly guilty.

"Well, I'm glad you're here!" she said emphatically, looking around to see if Blaine had finished talking with his guests. Their eyes met across the room, and noticing Josie talking to a handsome stranger, Blaine grew anxious and restless. "Excuse me, I must get back to my date. My agent can handle things and schedule meetings for us in the coming weeks," he explained and hurried over to Josie. "Sorry, honey," he said, then instinctively extended his hand to introduce himself, "Hi, I'm Blaine Cordwell. I don't think we've met?"

"You have, Blaine," said Josie. "This is Anthony Temple from my English Literature class. You met him a few months ago." Blaine was surprised by the dramatic change in the guy's appearance, especially since he had stirred Blaine's jealousy after Josie's class some months ago. "Wow, Anthony—you look sharp!" Blaine complimented Anthony, who felt uncomfortable as Blaine shook his hand a bit overenthusiastically, aware that Blaine was claiming his territory and warning him to back off. "Well, Josie, I'd better head home. I really am working on a writing project, and I need to finish it by next week," said Anthony timidly, his smile fading.

"Oh? Okay, Anthony," said Josie, aware of Blaine's aggression. "Thank you for rescuing me!" she said sincerely. "No problem," Anthony replied, offering a faint smile despite his growing dejection—he waved tentatively and blended into the crowd. "You didn't have to act like a caveman!" Josie snapped at Blaine, frustrated by his rude possessiveness.

"I'm sorry," Blaine apologized half-heartedly, "But I want to give you the surprise I promised you, right NOW!" he grinned. "What? Now?!" she blared, confused by the sudden expectation being demanded of her. "Yes, NOW!" Blaine insisted, taking Josie by the hand and hurrying her up a staircase to the roof of the exhibition center. "What are you doing, Blaine?" Josie asked, trying to catch her breath. "You'll see," he teased playfully as they approached a door that Blaine pushed open... to reveal a trail of red rose petals leading to the string quartet that had earlier played downstairs, now entertaining their private audience, framed by hundreds of Japanese lanterns hanging in an arch. Josie was captivated. "Blaine," she said, fighting back tears, "This is beautiful."

"I'm glad you like it. I wanted to recreate the night we first kissed in Haven Cove on the hood of my car under the Milky Way," he said with a smile. "This is so beautiful," Josie said, admiringly and slowly soaking in the scene. As the string quartet started to play **"Feels Like Heaven"** by Fiction Factory, Josie fought back tears. Blaine gently took her hand and led her to the center of the arch, wrapping his arms around her as they slow-danced under the Japanese lanterns. When the song ended, Blaine released her and knelt on one knee. Josie was stunned as Blaine gazed lovingly at her and opened a small black case. Inside was a breathtaking garnet ring surrounded by diamonds. "Meeting you, Josie, changed my life. For the first time, I feel truly alive, and I believe you entered my life for a reason — that we are destined to be together. I love you, Josie and the Pussycats. I always will — that's why I'm asking: Will you marry me?" Josie's heart was pounding; she immediately knew the answer to his question, but she wanted to savor the moment. Confused by the delay, Blaine waited patiently for her answer. She eventually broke into a beaming smile and unreservedly proclaimed, "Yes! Of course: YES!"

Blaine quickly stood up, slipped the ring onto her finger, and kissed her passionately. The quartet then broke into a rendition of Modern English's "**Melt with You,**" the song that serenaded them under the stars when they first kissed. As the crowd cheered, Blaine and Josie paused their kiss to acknowledge Blaine's mom and dad, who witnessed the touching moment. He was still in his wheelchair, having taken the elevator to the roof, and was now whistling happily. Josie giggled and turned back to face Blaine. "As I said over a year ago, Blaine—I see the real you, and I love you for it." Blaine chuckled, "Shut up, Josie—and kiss me," he said, pulling her close to finish their kiss as Blaine's parents kept cheering them on loudly as they embraced beneath the Japanese Lanterns—their own personal Milky Way. Josie wished this perfect moment would never end.

In the shadows, a woman growled as she squeezed her glass so tightly that it shattered in her hand. "We'll see whether you make it down the aisle, Josie!" Adeline spat, blood beginning to seep from the shards of glass in her hand. "Now look at what you made me do!" she muttered softly, making sure she wasn't heard. She grabbed her scarf, wrapped it snugly around her hand, and slipped away through the staff exit, unnoticed.

As Blaine wrapped his arms around Josie and pointed to the stars above, she noticed a shooting star streak across the sky. Blaine also saw the meteor. "It seems our love has always been written in the stars …" he said. "And inked in destiny," Josie added as they looked into each other's eyes and kissed once more, disregarding the audience of well-wishers who had appeared on the rooftop. This was their night to remember and treasure forever!

Later that night at Anthony's apartment ...

Anthony stood shirtless in front of the bathroom mirror, angrily splashing water on his face. "Don't be angry, my boy," he heard as he looked into the mirror and saw Alaric standing behind him. "I promised you the girl and the number one horror book in the country. And Alaric always keeps his promises," he said slyly, speaking about himself in the third person to add some objectivity.
"Well, Blaine has other ideas," Anthony countered as he dried his face with a towel and walked away, with Alaric trailing behind him like a dark shadow.

Alaric, I really don't want your company tonight," Anthony rudely remarked as he sat down at his Whitlock typewriter. "I have work to do," Anthony continued, putting on his glasses after earlier removing his contact lenses. Alaric walked over and sat in the chair by the window. "You know, Anthony ... the Whitlock Retreat is less than a week away."

"Yes, Alaric, I know," said Anthony angrily as he inserted a new sheet of paper into the typewriter carriage. "Now, if you would give me some space, maybe I can finish your story in time!" Anthony argued, hitting a button on his cassette player.

Jesus and Mary Chain's "**Halfway to Crazy**" came on, and Anthony cranked it up LOUD. "DO YOU REALLY NEED THAT DAMN NOISE TO LISTEN TO?" Alaric screeched, clutching his hands over his ears. Anthony turned to Alaric and brazenly responded, "Don't you have some writers to torture?" Alaric got up and walked over to the full-length mirror. "Anthony, just remember ..." he threatened menacingly, "I can crush your heart just by looking at you. Don't ever talk to me like that again, or you'll wish you were never born!" he growled as he waved his hand and the dark portal to the Realm of Darkness opened. Screams of torture met him as he stepped through the mirror and vanished.

Anthony exhaled in relief. Finally, he could focus on finishing Alaric's story and move forward, he thought, as he began typing while recalling how stunning Josie looked that evening—and that she would be his once he completed Alaric's tale. All he needed to do was tell this creature's story, and the world and Josie would fall at his feet. Anthony typed frantically through the night, dawn catching him slumped over the Whitlock typewriter, having fallen asleep with visions of Josie in her black gown and her admiration for him when he rescued her from those nasty piranhas.

Chapter Nine

<u>THE PROMISE</u>

Josie woke up to a flood of bright, white light filling the room. "Josie? Josie! Wake up!" She opened her eyes to see Eleanor standing beside her bed in the guest room at the Cordwell mansion. "Eleanor?" Josie croaked groggily, rubbing her eyes. "What's going on?" she asked. Eleanor, a vision of beauty with her long, blonde, cascading hair, wore an elegant white skirt suit and smiled as she sat down on the bed beside Josie.

Josie sat up. "Hi Eleanor, I'm sorry I'm not more alert," she said, yawning. "What time is it? Five?" "Josie, I don't have much time. Congratulations on your engagement to Blaine," she said, smiling. "I have a special gift for you," she added, gently placing a sealed letter into Josie's hands. "What's this?" Josie asked curiously, looking disheveled with her hair barely in a collapsed bun. "Open it and see," Eleanor said excitedly. Josie smiled as she carefully opened the gold envelope and pulled out a beautifully handwritten letter, the ink shimmering magically on the page. She also examined an antique key she found in the envelope. "Oh, you'll need to take this to the retreat, where Room 13 will reveal more answers for you... but put that key away for now; just make sure you take it with you," Eleanor said intriguingly. "Okay, I'll do that," Josie promised, tucking the key into her handbag on the bedside table beside her. "Now, Josie," Eleanor continued eagerly, "Please read the letter." As Josie unfolded the letter, tears welled in her eyes as she read aloud.

My Dearest Josie,

Congratulations, my darling, on your engagement to Blaine. Just imagine, I was watching over you two last night, glowing with pride. I'm so sorry I couldn't be there in person to tell you. I believe that writing to you is the next best thing, and thanks to Eleanor, I know this letter will reach you safely.

I remember when you were born—so tiny, with a thick mat of black, curly hair and your beautiful smile as you wrapped your hand around my finger. Your mother and I loved you before you were even born. Watching you grow up from afar has been the hardest thing for me as a father. I can't talk to you or your mother, but I stand silently observing, living your lives with you.

The hardest part of being a dad has been watching you grow up unnoticed. But Blaine has surprised me with his kindness, compassion, and dedication to you, and I was excited when Eleanor visited to share the good news.

I know the Whitlock Writer's Retreat is happening soon, but you two need to be very careful. Eleanor has promised to keep a close watch on both of you! As for Alaric, he needs to be stopped, and I believe you, Blaine, and Eleanor are the ones to do it.

Whenever you see a shooting star, think of me—it's a sign that I'm nearby!

I love you to the moon and back, my darling.
DAD!
XXOO

Josie set the letter down, and no sooner had she burst into tears than the bedroom door swung open, revealing Blaine standing there in the doorway, wearing boxer shorts and a Jane's Addiction T-shirt. "Eleanor! What are you doing here?" he asked, more surprised than the women were, then smirking. He closed the door and moved toward Josie. "What's going on, baby?" he asked with concern, noticing the tears on Josie's cheeks, which she quickly wiped away. "It's okay, Blaine, Eleanor has come to personally deliver an engagement present to us."

"Good morning, Blaine. I needed to deliver an important message from Josie's father," Eleanor explained, smiling warmly. Josie politely handed Blaine the letter. He sat on the bed to read it quietly to himself and, truly moved and astonished, exclaimed, "WOW! I didn't know someone who had passed away could still write," trying to add some levity to the moment. Eleanor smiled, "You're quite the comedian, aren't you, Blaine? ... I must get back to the Writers' Realm, though." She leaned into Josie and hugged her. "Congratulations again, you two—you make a wonderful couple." Eleanor briefly but affectionately embraced Blaine before turning to the mirror and softly brushing her hand across it; a warm, pulsating light radiated from its surface. "I'll be seeing you at the Whitlock retreat," she said as she entered the mirror and disappeared.

Blaine and Josie smiled warmly as they stood to see Eleanor off. Once she left, Blaine pulled Josie into his arms, then gently guided her onto the bed and hugged her close—intimately. "Blaine, I have my own surprise," Josie confessed, ... "And I was going to give it to you last night," she added. Blaine watched her with curiosity as she released their embrace to take a small gold-colored package from her bag, where she'd earlier put the key, and handed the little parcel to him. She giggled as he tore the wrapping paper open. A cassette tape emerged with the title:

BLAINE'S ARTISTIC INSPIRATION MIXTAPE

He smiled as he held his first gifted mixtape and kissed the top of Josie's head. "You're welcome," she said, acknowledging his gratitude. "I thought it was about time I made you a mixtape." "Well, it's going into my car stereo as soon as possible," said Blaine excitedly. They lay together, watching the rays of sunrise dance across the room's walls. Josie paused and turned to Blaine. "I know you're not going to take me seriously, but I need you to promise me something," she whispered. Blaine tilted his head forward, now serious. "Anything, Josie. You name it." "Promise me that if anything happens to me, you will remarry and move on with your life," she said, filled with heartache. "JOSIE! I CAN'T PROMISE YOU THAT!" Blaine protested, raising his voice; his face suddenly flushed with exasperation. Josie sat upright, her eyes wide and shimmering with urgency, her hands trembling slightly as she reached out. "Blaine, I need you to promise me this. It's important," she implored, voice shaking; her brows knitted with concern.

"WHY, Josie?! Why are you talking like this? We're just starting, and you're already talking about the end?!" Blaine's voice softened as confusion set in. He briefly looked away, running a hand through his hair, trying to understand her words. "Because life is short, Blaine! Look at my dad?" Josie said bravely, trying to be practical, though her eyes' glossiness betrayed her pain and unshed tears as she clenched her fist with restrained grief. "Josie, I'm not your dad ..." Blaine reassured her gently with a calming voice. Josie steadied herself. "Just hear me out ... I've had to watch my mom mourn my father's death every day for years ... and I don't want that for you," she explained, voice cracking as she reached out despairingly, her body trembling slightly. Blaine hesitated, silence hanging between them like a tense chord. Then he slowly nodded, swallowing hard. "Alright, I know what you mean ... so just to make you happy—*I promise!* —Okay?" His shoulders sagged as he looked into her pleading eyes, a faint smile finally breaking through his troubled demeanor. "And you do the same! Now stop talking like that—we just got engaged."

Josie's frown shifted into a wide smile, brightened by soft waves of relief and happiness spreading across her face. "Okay, I just needed to hear that because I love you too much to be a miserable memory to you …" Blaine thought they had dwelled on this awkward and terrible topic long enough, so he changed the subject. "You know you're blessed to have received that message from your dad. I think this is the first time I've ever heard of a deceased relative writing a letter," he implied.

Genuine curiosity filled the air as Josie smiled softly, snuggling close to him and letting her silky, flowing hair cascade onto his chest. "I know. The sad part is, I can't share it with my mom," she lamented, but that sentiment inspired Blaine to action. "Speaking of your mother, shouldn't we call her and share the good news?" Josie's face brightened for a moment, but glancing at the clock, she realized it was too early to call anyone. "Blaine, it's only six in the morning—let's give it a couple more hours."

"Okay, okay," he agreed as Josie rolled back over, affectionately draping his arm around her waist and gazing into her eyes. "So, what should I and the future Missus Cordwell do today?"
"That sounds so strange!" Josie giggled.
"Well, you'd better get used to it," Blaine declared as he began tickling Josie.

"Blaine? ... STOP!" Josie demanded sharply. "Can you smell something?" She turned around, trying to find the source of the burning smell, and both saw smoke curling up from the top drawer. "Crap!" Blaine yelled as he lifted Josie away and quickly grabbed a towel to pry open the top drawer, revealing a small fire inside. *"Josie, quick, hand me the pitcher of water on the dressing table!"* Josie, wearing her short top and shorts, snatched the pitcher and rushed to Blaine's side, flames roaring out of the drawer. *SPLASH*! She instinctively poured water onto the fire, and the flames died down instantly. Smoke now poured out of the drawer and soon triggered the smoke alarm. *"Quick!"* Blaine said as he opened the external sliding door, letting in the sea air, and the piercing alarm echoed throughout the house.

The internal door suddenly swung open—and Blaine's mom, panicked, yelled, "WHAT'S GOING ON, BLAINE?!"
"It's okay, Mom—one of Josie's candles tipped over. Everything's fine ..." Blaine stepped up to his mom and hugged her. "It's okay! I've got the situation under control," he said softly, kissing her furrowed brow. "Alright," she responded, her breathing slowing. "No more candles, Miss Josie," she said firmly. In shock, Josie went along with the cover-up.

"Sorry, Missus Cordwell," Josie apologized, amused by the thought that Blaine had just called her the same thing a minute ago. Blaine's mom shook her head as she kissed her son's cheek, then did it again before closing the door. The smoke alarm was soon silenced by the fresh salt air sweeping through the room. Blaine looked at Josie, curious, then asked the obvious question, "What caught fire?" They carefully examined the drawer and saw that the invitation to The Whitlock Estate Retreat was slightly scorched at the edges but otherwise unharmed, with no fire damage. "Look, Blaine," Josie said, pointing to a new message written in glowing red ink:

Two might plan to become one,

But following the Whitlock Writers' Retreat,

Josie and Blaine's relationship will be undone!

– Alaric

Stunned, Josie sat on the bed. "You mean Alaric did this to torment us?" she realized, feeling uneasy. "Josie ..." Blaine calmly began, "He knows he's headed for destruction, and so he's trying to psych us out. Don't let him win," he added, giving her a quick, encouraging kiss.

"Remember last night—our love is written in the stars..." he said emotionally. "And inked in destiny!" Josie finished with a smile as Blaine pulled her back onto the bed and kissed her passionately. Then, with clear intent, he declared, "No one! And I mean NO ONE, Josie, is going to stop us from being together—okay?!"

"How did I get so lucky?" she asked rhetorically. Blaine grinned excitedly. "Come on—let's go make pancakes for a celebration breakfast with my parents—and to apologize for nearly burning the house down!" he joked as he headed toward the open doorway. Motioning with one arm while holding the other behind his back, he mimicked a British accent— "After you, future Missus Cordwell." Josie smiled incredulously as the couple headed out, closing the bedroom door behind them.

The bedroom was filled with early-morning sunlight when the alarm clock shattered the silence, its loud ring slicing through like a sharp knife. Local morning radio hosts provided a traffic update before playing the next song on their playlist — **"The Promise"** by When in Rome. The radio and music were not the only things in the room, however. Hidden inside the ornate, antique dresser mirror, Aleric's ghostly form snarled in disgust as his ethereal face flickered and gradually faded into the glass. The mirror shuddered violently, and Aleric screamed in rage, his eyes shining with malice as he slipped back into the shadowy Realm of Darkness.

Chapter 10

<u>BEHIND THE WHEEL</u>

Whitlock Estate Writers' Retreat

Josie and Blaine drove silently for half an hour along winding roads bordered by tall gums and gnarled oaks; the forest grew darker and denser the higher they climbed. They were nervous; it was time to confront the secret society and discover what they truly wanted with Josie and her writing talent. Blaine turned on the car stereo to calm his nerves and pressed play. The familiar sounds of Depeche Mode's **"Behind the Wheel"** came to life from the mixtape Josie had given him. They listened nervously to the well-known song as Josie's pulse kept pace with the road markers flashing by on the isolated gravel road. Blaine's hand reached for hers, offering reassurance that everything would be fine.

The Whitlock estate suddenly appeared with towering spires full of hidden secrets. A vast, ivy-covered mansion clung to the edge of a cliff as if it had been carved from the stone itself. Its tall, narrow windows faintly glowed from within, like cats' eyes waking from a long sleep. The imposing wrought-iron gates—featuring a prominent uppercase 'W' and a family crest—were open when Josie and Blaine arrived. They hesitated slightly as they drove in along a long driveway lined with pencil willows, stopping at a designated guest parking area near the grand entrance to the manor.

They weren't alone: six cars were already parked there, and some young adults were unloading luggage from their vehicles and heading toward the building. Josie and Blaine sat in their car, watching the scene. "You know, Josie, I'm expecting the Scooby-Doo Mystery Machine to show up any minute now." Josie turned to Blaine. "What would I do without your wonderful sense of humor?" she said, amused, touching his cheek and then leaning in to kiss him.

Blaine and Josie finally stepped out of the car and grabbed their two lightly packed duffel bags from the trunk. Josie took a slow breath and said, "Here we go—into the lion's den." Blaine squeezed her hand tightly and whispered, "Remember, we're in this together, okay?" Josie smiled as Blaine's dark chestnut brown hair shimmered with strawberry highlights in the sunlight. He wore a Joy Division T-shirt under his black leather jacket, decorated with band pins; his trusty cherry Dr. Martens finished the look.

Josie wore black ripped denim jeans for the occasion, topped with a Cure 'Boys Don't Cry' T-shirt and a black corduroy jacket. Her hair was pulled back into a pigtail, and they wore matching sunglasses. The couple exuded post-punk chic as they casually walked up the path holding hands, their bags slung over their shoulders, toward the double oak doors that looked like they belonged on a medieval castle. The estate carried the scent of old parchment and salt, hints of buried secrets, and lingering things. A woman in her late 60s stood in the doorway, her churlish demeanor evident in the lack of a greeting smile. "Welcome," she said indifferently, her voice crisp and wooden. "I am Ms. Alder, the House Manager, Historian, and … let's say, I'm a guardian of the Whitlock legacy." She led them inside.

Josie and Blaine followed her as the oak doors closed behind them. From the entryway, they were guided into a grand library filled with velvet-cushioned chairs, walnut tables, Chesterfield sofas, and recliners. A massive bookcase lined the walls, holding thousands of volumes—mostly literary classics. Bright books with emerald, ruby, and sapphire bindings lined the shelves, their spines shining like gems in the light. *The Great Gatsby* by F. Scott Fitzgerald, *Mrs. Dalloway* by Virginia Woolf, and *Brave New World* by Aldous Huxley caught Josie's eye as she admired their beautiful leather bindings. The room glowed with warm golden lamplight, reflecting off polished walnut shelves that rose to a coffered ceiling decorated with intricate gilded geometric patterns. Brass sconces shaped like sunbursts decorated the spaces between the shelves, casting gentle, symmetrical shadows.

In the center, plush sofas and club chairs in luxurious cherry reds and chestnut browns formed an intimate circle around a sleek black marble coffee table with chrome edges. A soft cream rug underneath softened the room's angles, while crystal decanters on a mirrored tray sparkled invitingly.

On one side, an elegant Art Deco bar with an onyx countertop and mother-of-pearl inlays glowed softly under hidden lighting. Behind it, etched-glass shelves showcased fine liquors and stylish cut-glass tumblers, each a work of art. The air carried a subtle scent of leather, aged paper, oak, and a hint of cognac.

In a corner, a glossy black grand piano reflected the flowing architecture of the room. Soft jazz melodies drifted from hidden speakers, enveloping the space in a timeless, indulgent atmosphere: a haven for thinkers, lovers, and dreamers. "Josie?" She removed her sunglasses, surprised to see Anthony Temple sitting on a leather sofa near the large, unlit fireplace. He stood up and approached. "Josie?!" he exclaimed with delight. "Anthony! What are you doing here?" she asked innocently as she greeted him with a big hug. He smiled and reached into his pocket. "I was invited, of course," he replied, fishing his ticket from the pocket inside his jacket.

Blaine pulled Josie aside and whispered in her ear, "I don't like this, Josie."

"Be nice ..." she said through gritted teeth, "... It's good to see a friend," wrapping her arm around Blaine. Anthony stepped forward and shook Blaine's hand warmly. "Hi, Blaine. I didn't know you were an artist *and* a writer?"

"I'm not," he replied, trying to hide his jealousy. "I was invited because I'm Josie's fiancé."
"Oh," Anthony said, hiding his heartache. "Well, congratulations," he said generously as he invited them to sit beside him on the vintage Deco leather sofa near the fireplace. Josie and Blaine looked around. "Who are the others?" Josie whispered into Anthony's ear. "I don't know, Josie. There haven't been any formal introductions yet."

Presently, Ms. Alder returned. "It seems everyone is here. Welcome to the prestigious Whitlock Writers' Retreat for talented young writers. Please introduce yourselves while I step out to finalize our lunch arrangements," she said, closing the library doors with a faint smile as she left. A thin girl, barefoot and wearing a kaftan, spoke up. "I'll go first. My name is Evie Monroe, and I'm from Perth, Western Australia. I'm 18, and I love writing poetry," she said excitedly. "This is the first time I've been overseas, and receiving this invitation—

all expenses paid—is a dream come true," she added with a childish giggle. Her hauntingly dark-brown eyes looked innocently back at the group; her curly, strawberry-blonde hair framed her face.

"Well, I guess I'll go next," said a young man also dressed in a corduroy jacket, but he wore horn-rimmed glasses, and his hair was slicked back with gel. "My name is Theo Radcliffe, and I'm from Oxford, UK. I love cold, clinical thrillers, and I am currently studying a master's degree in Literary History and Politics at Oxford University," he announced most earnestly. He was holding a notebook and appeared intelligent, cynical, pragmatic, and quite secretive.

"Well, now it's my turn," said a young woman with long bleached blonde hair and white designer sunglasses. "My name is Marla Quinn. Yes, you all know me from *General Hospital,* but I've become an author. I'm twenty-four years old, from Los Angeles, and I write screenplays and dramatic monologues," she informed the group, smiling sweetly. But behind that fake smile, Josie could see a snake—the type of woman who demands attention when she enters a room.

"Hey, I know you," she said to Blaine, removing her white sunglasses and leaning forward suddenly in her club chair, like a mischievous schoolgirl. "You're Blaine Cordwell. Oh my, we have a rock star's son here, folks!" she announced excitedly. All eyes briefly turned to Blaine in awkward silence until Josie stepped in. "Hi, my name is Josie, and this is Blaine, my fiancé. I'm studying journalism, and Blaine is a talented artist who just held his first art exhibition," she explained. Blaine added, "Hi, everyone, I'm just Blaine. Yes, my dad's Dean Cordwell, but I'm my own person," he said firmly. Josie intervened, "So, we're both happy to meet you all," she said, trying to smooth things over. Blaine shifted uncomfortably on the sofa, thinking about grabbing Josie's hand and rushing out of the room, leaving Whitlock Estate. Still, he kept his composure, channeling his frustration toward Alaric and their mission to remove him from their lives once and for all.

Hi, Blaine—We share a common interest. I'm also a musician. My name is Rowan Vega, and I'm from Barcelona. I enjoy writing lyrics and snippets of surreal prose in multiple languages." Blaine smiled back, "Hi, Rowan."

"So, I get it, man, it can be tough having a famous dad. My own father is very well known in Spa ..."

"BORING!" Marla interrupted, rudely cutting off Rowan mid-sentence. "NEXT!" she demanded. Josie frowned at Marla, making a mental note to avoid sitting near her during lunch and to stay away from her entirely. Instead of acknowledging Marla, she chose to oppose her by supporting her victim. "Nice to meet you, Rowan," Josie politely greeted the Spaniard, while frowning at Marla.

Anthony chimed in. "Hi, I'm Anthony Temple, and I'm studying journalism at USC. I know Josie and Blaine. I'm a huge Stephen King fan and love writing horror." Josie and Blaine looked at each other with concern, both thinking the same thing. "Could this be Alaric's new writer?" Blaine whispered to Josie. "Of course!" Josie replied knowingly. "Eleanor warned me that Alaric would choose someone I already knew ..."

"Excuse me!" Marla interrupted. "Both of you are being pretty rude to poor Anthony."
"Sorry," said Josie apologetically. "Continue, Anthony. We didn't mean to interrupt," Blaine immediately sought to make amends. "That's okay,

I've finished anyway," he said shyly, pushing his glasses up and looking down.

"Well, I guess I'm last," said a young man with a French accent. "My name is Silas Vale, and I won a Whitlock writing scholarship at the University of Montpellier in the South of France." He was dressed in gray and seemed polite enough, but as Josie watched, she sensed something was off and grew more suspicious of the other writers. He didn't seem genuine. Was Alaric haunting him too? Haunting everyone in this ragtag group of bohemian eccentrics? Her realization about Anthony made her paranoid. Just as Silas finished his introduction, the library doors swung open again, and Ms. Alder entered to stand before them. "Well, I'm glad to announce that lunch is served. Please leave your bags at the front entrance, and I will have the staff take them to your rooms. I will show you to your rooms after lunch," she said with a stern, dry smile.

"Wow," I feel like a millionaire," giggled Evie as the mismatched group slowly carried their bags back to the main entrance, talking among themselves. Josie and Blaine stayed at the back of the group. "Blaine, we need to keep our eyes on

Anthony and Silas," she said discreetly. Blaine turned to Josie and whispered, "Okay, Anthony, I can understand, but why Silas?"

"Because there's something too familiar about Silas, and that's making me very uncomfortable," she replied, interrupted by Ms. Alder's new directions. "If you make your way to the dining hall, your lunch is being served." Her tone was stern, almost comical, like Riff Raff from The Rocky Horror Picture Show, Josie thought, as the group of young writers shuffled down imposing, high corridors and into a grand dining room, leaving their luggage and the world behind them. Josie and Blaine were the last to follow. Realizing they had arrived at a critical moment, Blaine whispered to Josie, "Okay, Josie, we still have time to back out and leave ..."

"No, Blaine, we need to put an end to Alaric's interference in our lives once and for all," Josie responded confidently. "Okay, Josie and The Pussycats, here we go," Blaine affirmed with a determined smile, squeezing her hand.

She looked into Blaine's eyes and whispered, "Let's rock!" as they entered the viper's den; the doors to the room—and destiny—slamming shut behind them.

Chapter Eleven

<u>LOVE SONG</u>

Walking into the dining room was like entering a jewelry box filled with Art Deco treasures. Light from a grand geometric chandelier spread across mirrored walls, each reflection capturing the shimmer of gold leaf accents and polished chrome trim. A black-and-white marble floor extended beneath their feet in a bold chevron pattern, guiding the eye to a long, dark-lacquered wooden dining table, its glossy surface set with crystal goblets and porcelain plates rimmed in platinum. Velvet-upholstered chairs in deep emerald encircled the table; their curved backs edged with brass studs that shimmered like tiny stars.

The air carried a subtle scent of polished mahogany and fresh lilies arranged in a tall, fluted vase at the center of the table, where it served as a sculptural focal point. Tall windows framed by flowing silk drapes let in soft afternoon light, diffused by frosted glass panels etched with stylized sunbursts.

Symmetrical patterns were common, featuring sharp, angular shapes or dramatic curves; bold contrasts and rich textures filled the space, yet the atmosphere remained warm and cinematic, enhanced by barely audible cocktail jazz beneath the gentle murmur of conversations and the clinking of champagne flutes. All the other writers were seated, and Josie and Blaine took their places at their name cards on the table; two spots remained at the head of the table for the hosts of the Writers' Retreat.

The room buzzed with excitement and anticipation, but Josie knew more about this secret society than the other writers had been told. They built Alaric to gain power, control, and dominance over talented writers, forcing them to complete stories using their signature Whitlock typewriters and magical ink, which brought whatever the writers created to life in the realms of light or darkness.

Their stories and characters were no longer just fictional; they had taken on a life of their own in the spiritual realm, unknown to their author. If an author died with an unfinished manuscript, a Whitlock Society Writer would complete it so the story remained whole, and their characters could continue living in another realm. Josie didn't understand why she was called to attend, but she felt compelled to go. They clearly had writers from around the world willing to do anything for fame and success in the literary world. So why her, and why was Blaine supposed to attend with her?

"Ladies and gentlemen," announced Ms. Alder in a formal tone. "I am pleased to introduce your hosts for the weekend, Ms. Seraphina McBell and Mr. Tyler Franklin, long-time members of the *Whitlock Society of Literary Excellence,* whose mission is to promote the writers of tomorrow. Please stand," Ms. Alder ordered.

The lively group quickly gathered around the table—Evie adjusted her skirt while Anthony busily fixed his tie. The oak doors swung open, revealing a striking woman in her 40s with long black hair, dressed in a sleek black-and-silver satin gown, with a fair complexion and ruby-red lips. She smiled like a '50s Hollywood starlet as she was escorted by a tall, handsome man with dark brown hair, a mustache, and piercing blue eyes. He wore a tuxedo.

They owned the room, radiating an aura of elegance, mystique, and suave sophistication as they approached the head of the table. Mr. Franklin carefully pulled out the chair for Ms. McBell to sit in. She wore a diamond-encrusted bracelet that twinkled brightly as she delicately placed a lace napkin on her lap. Mr. Franklin then took his place beside her. Ms. Alder roared, "Guests, please be seated."

The youngsters sat quickly, full of nervous excitement. Unsure of what to do next and waiting for their hosts, the room fell silent, nearly too quiet. Ms. McBell sensed the tension and broke it at just the right moment. "Dear guests, please relax and continue your conversations. Mr. Tyler and I are pleased that you all made the long journey to be here this weekend. Please enjoy your lunch." The group gradually and quietly resumed their conversations, so much so that when Ms. McBell and Mr. Franklin started talking, their words couldn't be heard, and soon, Tyler prompted a playful laugh from Seraphina.

Smirking, Blaine whispered to Josie, "Doesn't this remind you of an episode of The Addams Family?" Josie giggled in agreement, "Well, that would make me Wednesday Addams," she suggested. Blaine chuckled in agreement. "Then who am I?" he challenged her. After a moment, Josie realized she couldn't really compare him to Pugsley or Uncle Fester. "Because of your height, you would have to be Lurch," she concluded, thinking it was a funny comparison since they had almost nothing else in common. Blaine smiled, "Thanks, Josie," and they went back to enjoying the Great Gatsby vibe in the room.

Currently, waitstaff enter the hall with silver trays, carefully placing them in front of each guest. After all the trays are distributed, Mr. Franklin stands briefly and loudly announces, "Bon appétit," with a French accent. The waiters lift the silver domes on the trays to reveal a perfectly plated meal of rare roast beef, infused with garlic and rosemary to tantalize the senses, surrounded by freshly steamed garden vegetables and a side of red wine jus. "Well, this is definitely what I call fine dining," Blaine remarks as they both pick up their sterling silver cutlery and begin eating.

Blaine paused occasionally to look around the room, focusing on Anthony and Evie, who sat together and seemed to be enjoying each other's company. Her Australian accent was charming, and she giggled when Anthony tried to imitate it. Her beauty was striking, and her effortless, natural smile lit up the room. Josie also watched the couple, sensing sparks of romance between them. When she noticed they were being watched, Evie looked back at Josie and waved enthusiastically. Embarrassed that Evie had caught her observing them, Josie smiled politely and waved back.

Rowan Vega sat across from Blaine, and the two started discussing Spanish influences on modern musicians. They seemed to get along well, while on Josie's other side sat a quiet Silas Vale, the dark horse of the group who reminded her that sometimes things aren't as they appear. Silas was eating when Josie tried to start a conversation. "Silas? Please tell me more about yourself," she asked politely. He gently put his cutlery down and turned to Josie, giving her his full attention. "Well, Josie, I come from Montpellier, which is in southern France. I attend the University of Montpellier, one of the oldest universities in the world," he said. "Sounds amazing..." Josie responded reassuringly, focusing on his eyes.

"Yes, Josie, it is wonderful. The town has a beautiful 17th-century historic area called the "Écusson," with narrow cobbled streets, market courtyards, and street cafés," he said in a charming French accent as she picked up her knife and fork and continued eating, encouraging him to do the same. They talked about the treats available at those charming patisseries and cafés tucked around every little street corner, as well as the university's botanical gardens, which are among the oldest in France.

Watching the growing restlessness at the table as most of the guests finished eating, Mr. Franklin once again stood to make another announcement. "You all must be exhausted from your travels. Ms. Alder will show you to your rooms, and then you're welcome to explore our beautiful gardens and library until we meet here again at 6 p.m. for dinner." He helped Ms. McBell up, offering his hand politely. She smiled warmly at the group and said, "We are so looking forward to getting to know you all—our talented new Whitlock Writers! Spend the afternoon exploring the grounds and getting to know each other," she advised, as she wrapped her arm around Tyler's. Ms. Alder clapped and encouraged the teens to stand and pay tribute to their welcoming guests as they left the dining room. The oak doors closed behind them. "Please come with our staff and me to take your bags to your rooms," Ms. Alder now directed, leading the group toward the door.

Josie and Blaine deliberately lagged behind, being the last to gather their belongings at the entrance. "Our staff will show you all to your rooms," Ms. Alder instructed. As she spoke, two men and two women in black-and-white waitstaff uniforms led the teens up the grand, sweeping mahogany staircase, with Ms. Alder leading and pausing to face them as they ascended. The nearby wall was decorated with numerous old black-and-white photos. "As you can see, hanging on the wall are our annual portraits of previous young writers who have attended this retreat over the years," Ms. Alder told the group. Josie and Blaine noticed that the retreat dates back to the early 1900s. "Josie, look!" exclaims Blaine as he points to a framed photo of a retreat in Haven Cove, with Eleanor and June front and center. Josie stops and looks at the two young people from Haven Cove, writers in their early 20s—beautiful, smiling, and waving for the camera—with a Whitlock typewriter in front of them. "Josie!" Blaine calls out, pointing to a tall, dark shadow behind the women in the photo. The color drains from Josie's face as she recognizes who it was—"Alaric!" she whispers.

"Come, you two—stop straggling!" Ms. Alder urged them along, still the last people on the staircase. "Sorry," Josie apologized half-heartedly and offered a made-up excuse: "Blaine and I just love photography." Ms. Alder quietly mumbled something to herself, then turned away at the top of the stairs and kept going, Blaine and Josie following her down a long corridor where most of the group had already been shown to their rooms. Soon, they stopped outside a door. "This is where you will be staying, Blaine," Ms. Alder said, motioning him in as she opened the door to a suite. "Your room is next door, Josie, and there'll be no hanky-panky! Is that understood?!"
"Yes, ma'am! I wouldn't dream of it," Josie sheepishly assured the lady of her good intentions.

Ms. Alder left Josie with a firm warning: "Dinner is at 6 p.m. sharp! Dress formally and don't be late!" as she closed the door behind her. Josie dropped her bags and stepped into a bedroom that felt frozen in a glamorous dream, lost in time. The space was lavishly and elegantly decorated in the Art Deco style—a world of symmetry, sparkle, and quiet sophistication. The walls were paneled in glossy ebony and ivory, interrupted by large windows along the exterior wall, and a glass door led to a small balcony. Large paintings and mirrors adorned the remaining walls, framed in gilded wood and sunburst patterns that caught the light of a low crystal chandelier. A geometric chevron-patterned rug stretched across the shiny hardwood floor, with muted greens and deep blacks anchoring the room with bold clarity.

At the center of the back wall, a grand four-poster bed made of polished walnut with gilded inlays rose like a stage. Chiffon drapes in a soft champagne hue hung from the frame, highlighting the blood-red velvety pillows and silky sheets beneath a gold-patterned cream bedspread. A vanity with a curved glass top gleamed in one corner, its chrome accents reflecting the glow of twin alabaster lamps shaped like stylized torches. On the opposite wall, tall windows framed in heavy jade drapery overlooked a distant town. The fabric, embroidered with subtle metallic threads, shimmered as Josie moved closer. The entire room seemed to hum with quiet confidence, blending luxurious theatricality with reclusive intimacy—a sanctuary for sharing secrets whispered in the night.

Ms. Alder had just stepped down the stairs when Blaine knocked on Josie's door. She let him in, and they quickly became part of the room's lively tapestry and charm. "Wow!" Josie squealed, twirling before collapsing face down onto the bed, giggling and rolling over. "I feel like I'm in *The Great Gatsby!*" she declared as Blaine joined her on the bed. Sitting comfortably, the couple cuddled, admiring their surroundings and enjoying the lovely lavender scent drifting into the room through the open windows.

"You know, Blaine," said Josie, "We might be in a viper's den, but I have to say—I feel like I'm the star of a novel." Blaine smirked, "Once a writer, always a writer," he quipped as he gently pressed her face with a heavy black and gold paisley-embroidered pillow filled with feather down. She responded with a more forceful whack of the cushion to the side of his head, and several minutes of playful pillow fights followed, with Josie falling into Blaine's arms and kissing him passionately.

"Wait!" Blaine suddenly said before sitting up and rushing out of her room. "What are you doing?" Josie asked herself, giggling and confused. Blaine quickly returned, playfully pulling out a small, portable cassette player. Josie laughed, "When did you pack that?!"

"When you weren't looking. Desperate times call for desperate measures, and we can't go without our music." Josie's laughter faded as he placed the device on the drawer beside her and leaned in again to kiss her, now with The Cure's **"Love Song"** softly playing in the background. Perfect, Josie thought as she kissed Blaine, lost in the moment surrounded by beautiful scenery, luxury, '80s music, and the love of her life. Life couldn't get any better, she thought, oblivious to the gardens or the others in the group as they spent the afternoon talking, laughing, and simply enjoying each other's company—being a newly engaged couple—completely unaware of the danger lurking behind the vintage mirror in her room!

Chapter Twelve

<u>THE RIDDLE</u>

The last golden rays of daylight streamed through the French louvers on her window as Josie stirred. She opened her eyes, groggily awakening to find Blaine snuggled right beside her. She lifted her arm to check her watch: it was 5:50 p.m. "CRAP!" she exclaimed, turning to Blaine. "Wake up! Wake up, Blaine," she said, as he slowly opened his eyes. "Josie?"

"We have ten minutes to get dressed for dinner, and it's formal attire!" she exclaimed, panic creeping into her voice as she hurriedly leapt off the bed. Blaine, still half asleep, rolled over sluggishly and closed his eyes again. "BLAINE!" Josie snapped, her voice sharper now. He opened one eye with a groan. "Okay, okay, I'm getting up," he mumbled, fumbling unsteadily to his feet and walking back to his room. Josie hurriedly unpacked her formal dress, slipping into it quickly and confidently. Blaine managed to gather enough energy to move quickly. It was 5:58 p.m. when Blaine and Josie left their rooms and hurried down the corridor in a panic, rushing down the winding, grand staircase. Josie tied her hair into a bun as they approached the dining room. Blaine chuckled when he looked over at Josie and saw her zipper open at the back. Josie looked at him in disbelief. "Stop," he said. "Turn around." She followed his instructions, confused until he zipped up her dress. "Thanks," Josie said gratefully, relieved that Blaine had noticed the mistake. "You're welcome, madam," Blaine said, adopting his best posh English accent again in jest, smiling charmingly. "Okay, you are pretty amazing," she said as he extended his arm for her to take as they headed to the dining room.

It was 6:02 p.m. when Josie and Blaine reached the closed oak doors of the dining room. "Here we go again," Blaine said as they pushed the doors open and entered. All the guests were seated, and Ms. Alder was standing at a microphone to the side of the room. The dining room looked stunning, but with everyone's eyes on the latecomers, the banquet hall temporarily felt more like a courtroom.

As Blaine and Josie neared the table, a heavy atmosphere filled the room, heightened by the symmetry of the decor, the cold shine of glass and silver, and the intentionally subdued mood. It was as if every fork, candle, and petal of the stark white lilies had been deliberately arranged for a purpose beyond basic hospitality.

The mirrored runner in the center of the table reflected the guests, slightly distorting their images and making it seem as if the room itself was watching and testing them. High-backed chairs flanking the table added an eerie presence, as if unseen figures were lingering just out of sight. The chandeliers above gently hummed; their crystals cast fractured beams that appeared to follow movement like spotlights.

When Blaine shifted, the light moved across him, highlighting his body before plunging him into shadow again. Josie sensed eyes behind the mirrors on the wall, unseen watchers scrutinizing her every gesture and assessing her strengths and weaknesses. This wasn't just a dinner table; it was a testing ground, an unspoken trial by candlelight where even sitting down felt like surrendering to an unseen force. A bar cart in the corner gleamed with crystal decanters and cut-glass tumblers, their facets catching the chandelier's glow. On the far wall, a mural of stylized silver cranes in flight soared against a midnight blue background, adding grandeur and motion to the room. The air carried a faint scent of waxed wood and expensive perfume—reminding that this space was meant for spectacle: secrets whispered over champagne, and eyes that lingered just a little too long across the table.

The young writers sat in different spots than they did at lunch. "Nice to see both of you found your seats," Ms. Alder said snidely, clearly annoyed by their tardiness. It looked like the organizers wanted to shuffle the group, as Josie was now sitting on one side of the table next to Theo and the obnoxious Marla. Meanwhile, Blaine sat opposite her, next to Silas on one side and Evie on the other.

Ms. Alder waited until *everyone* was comfortably seated. "Tonight, you will learn about the Whitlock Society and its importance in the literary world." Evie whispered to Blaine, "How exciting is this?" She laughed warmly. "Very exciting," Blaine replied sarcastically, but he still smiled through gritted teeth. Josie watched him, making sure he behaved without being told to do so under the table. He smiled sweetly at her, knowing what she was thinking. She smiled back, then looked away, turning her attention to Marla, whose eyes were fixed on Ms. Alder.

Before our esteemed hosts join us again, I have prepared a short instructional video covering everything you need to know. Dawson, please turn off the lights," she said, and the room dimmed as a projection screen lowered from the ceiling. Symbols flickered on the screen—a Celtic cross and other mysterious symbols—all synchronized with haunting music. A close-up of Ms. McBell suddenly filled the screen, impeccably made-up with her hair in an elegant bun. "Welcome, new writers. Before you begin your writing journey with us, you need to understand you are on a mission." The guests all looked at each other, puzzled. "Yes, that's right—you have a mission! The Whitlock Society's job is to ensure that good and evil stay in balance. We are not just a writing society, but a secret organization entrusted with this vital work for hundreds of years," she explained.

The first Whitlock Writer was an Indian author named Tesmar, who in 1832 wrote a horror story inspired by Indian folklore. However, Tesmar possessed a unique gift; he discovered that his fictional works connected to an alternate reality, where his stories became real and formed small universes within a supernatural dimension called the Writers' Realm. By learning about and even visiting this place, Tesmar created two types of stories: one for the Realm of Light, consisting of pure, golden, and heartwarming tales; and another for the dark realm of shadows—dark horror stories, murder mysteries, and other ominous themes. Each realm has a head editor who oversees and manages these hidden works. These other-dimensional worlds exist beyond our reality and coexist peacefully without interacting—each remaining quite distinct," said Ms. McBell in the video presentation. "In those worlds—the two realms— the characters are real and live out their stories without realizing they are fictional. It must stay that way," said Ms. McBell.

The group of teenagers looked stunned. Marla stood up. "I'm leaving! This makes no sense at all. I'm being pranked, right? Okay, guys, where's the camera crew? You're behind those glass mirrors, aren't you?" Josie got up. "Marla, this is all *true,*" she said flatly, grabbing Marla's attention. "Of course, *you'd* think that Josie and the Pussycats," she added with disdain, as she motioned to leave.

Ms. Elder turned off the screen. "BRADFORD?! SECURE THE DOORS!" she ordered. The oak doors were quickly bolted shut by a burly security officer who then took up guard at the passageway. Panic erupted, and all the visitors stood up from their chairs, ready for anything. "ENOUGH!" Blaine shouted firmly. "ALL OF YOU, SIT DOWN NOW!" Everyone slowly but nervously sat back down. Ms. Elder nodded to thank Blaine. He responded with a deliberate blink and a slight nod of his head before she addressed the group again. "Please relax ... no one will get hurt; everyone is safe, and you're all going home after this weekend—and yes, everything Ms. McBell said is true!" she reassured everyone.

"Josie and I can vouch for that," Blaine added, gesturing toward Josie, who was still seated and momentarily stunned by the chaos. Regaining her composure, she stood with Blaine, and Ms. Alder signaled downward with flat hands to quiet the group; Josie calmly said, "Everyone, please sit down. We will explain..."

Before Josie could speak again, Ms. McBell's voice echoed through the room. "Ladies and gentlemen, please remain calm." The panel of the glass-mirrored wall slid open, revealing a hidden doorway through which Seraphina and Tyler stepped, both dressed elegantly. The group sat in silence, wondering what other surprises the evening might hold, but they found some comfort in Seraphina's effortless grace.

She looked surprisingly relaxed in her fine clothing and carried an almost carefree attitude as she was escorted by the dashing Mr. Franklin to the head of the table. Tyler helped Seraphina with her chair and adjusted the tail of his coat, then sat down beside her. The room grew completely silent; all eyes were on their hosts. Seraphina looked at the group and spoke eloquently. "My dear guests, you all know you were brought here for a reason, and you've heard some strange things that may have challenged your perception of reality," she said.

Tyler interrupted, "Yes, quite so. But please be assured that we hold you all in the highest regard as highly talented writers, and we plan to nurture your skills this weekend. Now, Cook has informed me that she has prepared a lavish banquet, so let's enjoy our feast and then retire to the parlor for drinks and conversation." With a wave of her arm, Ms. Alder directed the security guard to allow the kitchen staff to bring their guests' meals into the dining room.

Josie looked around the room and noticed concern on the guests' faces; their suspicions were probably heightened by Bradford still standing guard at the door. Marla, sitting beside her and still in shock, murmured, "This must be a reality show." Evie looked upset until Blaine whispered something funny in her ear, causing her to chuckle. The guests' thoughts shifted to eating as their luxurious meals were brought out on silver trays; lifting the domed covers revealed veal scallopini with roasted vegetables and dinner rolls. "Bon appétit!" responded Tyler, urging his guests to eat.

Anthony remained calm, showing no signs of distress, while Silas kept busy chatting with Blaine as if nothing unusual had happened. Josie looked into Silas's eyes again, sensing that feeling of familiarity she'd noticed before, but she still couldn't identify it. Meanwhile, Theo focused on

Seraphina, who was talking casually with Tyler.

After dinner, Seraphina urged her guests to follow her to the parlor for refreshments and an explanation. As they rose, Blaine signaled for Josie to talk with Anthony and find out if Alaric had reached out to him. Anthony passed by her chair. "Anthony," she said sweetly, "Would you mind escorting me to the parlor?" Anthony stopped suddenly, surprised and pleased at the same time. "I would love to, Josie!" he replied warmly, offering his arm for her to take and making a quick, humorous remark that Josie responded to with a relaxed laugh as he led her out of the dining room. Always the gentleman, Blaine also offered Evie his arm to escort her, and they exited through the oak doors.

The parlor radiated elegance, blending luxury with intimacy. Black lacquered walls adorned with thin strips of polished brass reflected the warm glow of crystal sconces, their geometric shades casting fractured light across the room. A sweeping sunburst mirror hung above a marble fireplace; its gold rays radiated outward like a frozen explosion of light.

Velvet club chairs in jewel tones of emerald, sapphire, and deep garnet were arranged in conversational groups, with their low, gracefully curved backs inviting guests to sink in and linger. A long ivory sofa, edged in glossy black wood, anchored the room; its cushions accented by silk pillows with hand-stitched floral designs. The room's focal point was a stunning cocktail bar: a semicircular counter crafted from inlaid walnut and chrome, with mirrored shelves reflecting cut-glass decanters, crystal coupes, and slender-necked bottles glowing in amber and ruby beneath deco pendant lights. The air carried a subtle aroma of orange peel, tobacco, and French perfume.

Jazz played softly from a sleek gramophone in the corner, its lacquered horn catching the lamplight. On a low glass table, a crystal ashtray and a silver shaker gleamed next to a stack of cocktail napkins embroidered with tiny golden stars. Seraphina stood beside Tyler near a club chair, while the staff busily served red wine and whiskey. "Let's raise our glasses to the truth," Tyler proposed, and the room echoed with the clinking of glasses. Seraphina continued, "As I said in my video presentation, there are gifted writers in this world who can transform a simple story into an alternate reality." Marla was about to speak, but Seraphina rebuked her, sternly yet politely, "Marla, please ask questions once I'm finished." She continued, "There are special writers known as 'Conduits' who can turn fictional stories into new realms of reality where the characters believe they are real. I believe Josie and Blaine have had previous experience with this ability," she paused, now awaiting Josie's interjection ... "Oh yes, in Haven Cove, writers were disappearing, and one writer—Eleanor Wren—was murdered! Her soul was trapped in a Whitlock typewriter."

Murmurs and scoffs of disbelief greeted Josie's comment. Still, Seraphina insisted, "My dear guests, I can assure you this is reality, not fiction. So, before you choose to ridicule Josie and her partner Blaine, I suggest that after our meeting, you find out the truth!" she said with disdain. Tyler responded, "My dear," turning to Seraphina, "May I continue?" She nodded. "When a writer dies before such a special manuscript is finished, the writer's soul becomes trapped until a conduit—a gifted writer such as you all are—finishes the manuscript, releasing the soul and the story into the

Writers' Realm, where the fictional characters live out their lives unaware that they are products of a writer's imagination. We here at Whitlock Society believe you all have this special power, when combined with our own typewriters and special ink," he explained.

"What you need to understand is that this isn't fiction but fact. If the unfinished stories aren't released from limbo, our world could fall apart. Some of you have already met Alaric—a shadowy phantom from the Realm of Darkness who was once an ally of ours—but his pride led him down a dark path. He wants to have a physical body and will do anything to reach his goal," finished Tyler, swirling cognac in his glass, then taking a long sip.

"Excuse me?!" Theo snapped, clearly annoyed. "What proof do you have that any of this is true?" challenged the Oxford-educated skeptic.
"Good question," Tyler replied to Theo. "The proof will be shown to you all tomorrow, but you must stay in this retreat until your training is finished."
"What! Are you holding us here against our will?" Marla insinuated. "Not at all, Marla," Seraphina said soothingly, "But we strongly recommend you stay overnight, and training starts at 9 a.m.

tomorrow. That's all we can tell you for now. Enjoy your stay with us—Tyler and I will head out for the evening." With that, Tyler guided her out of the parlor, and the waitstaff closed the door behind them. "What just happened?" Evie asked, confused. Blaine, who had just been served whiskey on the rocks, turned to the group and declared, "Everything they said is true," taking a steady sip of bourbon. "It can't be," said Marla in shock. "Well, Marla, the truth is true, whether you believe it or not." Josie shot back, putting Marla in her place and a wry smile on Blaine's face, pleased that his fiancée had a way with words.

"Okay, listen," Blaine said casually as he wandered away from the bar toward Josie. "Last year, Josie and I were in the same situation as all of you are right now. We get it—all this is hard to believe— but it's true. Reality really can be stranger than fiction," he said. Theo nodded in agreement, surprisingly acknowledging Blaine's point that life can be extremely bizarre—even absurd at times— but, of course, Theo would need to see concrete proof of the outlandish claims being made. "Josie?" Evie began softly, "Can you please tell us exactly what is going on?" Sensing her distress,

Anthony gently rubbed Evie's arm for support, and she smiled at him, grateful for his personal touch. Josie took a deep breath. "There is another dimension that we have encountered, called the Writers' Realm, which holds authors in the afterlife, and their special stories—stories that come to life, where characters live in one of two realms: the Realm of Light, for uplifting, moral tales; and the Realm of Darkness, for horror and crime stories that indulge in fear and dread."

Marla shook her head. "Okay, guys, I'm going home!" she said as she stood up to leave. "SIT DOWN NOW, MARLA!" Josie barked, startling everyone. Blaine smirked, but he appreciated Josie's authoritative side when she meant business. "Now, before I was rudely interrupted by Marla, I was about to say Blaine and I have both seen these realms with our own eyes," said Josie.
"Yes, we have," Blaine added. "What Josie is saying is that all of you are talented writers for a reason, and that reason is to make sure unfinished stories are completed and released into the right realm," he explained. "Who is this Alaric character?" asked Rowan. "Well," Josie answered, "He is the Chief Editor in the Realm of Darkness,

which is basically hell for the souls of tormented writers who create in these dark genres."

"Josie—this is nonsense," Anthony interrupted unhelpfully. "No, Anthony," Blaine said firmly, "Alaric is real, and he's a bad guy! He wants a human body and needs one of you to help him get it."

"What do we get if we do it?" asked Marla. Evie interrupted, "Marla, would you really help a character equivalent to the devil for material gain?" "I sure would—if it meant I became rich and powerful," she said shamelessly.

"Are you saying you'd give up your soul just to show off a fancy handbag, Marla?" Josie asked incredulously. "Is the handbag Gucci?" Marla responded mockingly. Josie was angry and moved toward Marla to confront her. Blaine knew that look and held Josie back. "Hold your horses, Josie and the Pussycats," he said. "Blaine, let go of me!" Josie exclaimed angrily.

"ENOUGH!" Evie yelled. "We shouldn't be acting like this."

"I agree with Evie," said Theo. "I suggest we all call it a night and pick this up tomorrow after we've seen the evidence they say proves this is all true."

The group seemed pleased with Theo's conclusion. "Sounds good to me," said Rowan. Blaine noticed that Silas was quiet in the corner with an amused look on his face. "Silas?" asked Blaine. "Do you have anything to add?"

"Sorry, I just find it amusing when women fight. I agree we should all call it a night." The group finished their drinks, left their glasses on the bar, and slowly made their way out of the parlor and up the stairs. Along the way, they noticed two burly bodyguards standing guard at the front door.

Marla whispered to Evie, "So much for this not being a prison." Evie looked at the bodyguards. "At least they're kind of cute," Evie suggested to Marla, who responded with a soft, naughty chuckle. "I like you, Evie, even if I can't understand your Australian accent," said Marla as they all headed up the stairs along the corridor to their adjoining rooms. They casually said 'good night' to each other and entered their rooms, closing the doors behind them—all except Josie and Blaine, who stayed outside Blaine's door for a while.

"Wow, what a night!" Blaine exhaled. Josie felt relieved to get away from Marla. "Marla isn't going to last the weekend," she anticipated. Blaine smiled, "Why do you think I restrained you?" Josie smiled too, "Okay, okay, that woman just pushes my buttons." Blaine put his arms around Josie and kissed her neck. She giggled, "You know how to distract me." She pulled away from Blaine. "I'm going to take a shower and get into my pajamas." "Your passion killers?" Blaine asked.

"My passion killers are exactly what's needed until we're married," she said, poking her tongue out and then playfully pecking him on the lips.

Blaine shook his head. He admired Josie's strong morals and respected her for them. "Let's get some rest, and when everyone is asleep, we need to do some snooping," Josie proposed with a mischievous smile. "What are you working on, investigative reporter?" Blaine commented with a smile.

Josie said, "We need to find our own answers before tomorrow."

"All right, Josie, I'll leave my door unlocked. Wake me up when you're ready. I don't want you going alone, okay?" Josie tilted her head and said, "See, this is why I love you." Then she playfully kissed his nose, broke their embrace, and headed for her door. "Good night!" she teased before disappearing into her room. Blaine smiled, and once inside his room, he quickly changed out of his formal clothes into his boxer shorts and a Clash T-shirt. He jumped into bed, exhausted.

Josie briefly turned on her portable cassette player in her room, keeping the volume low. She settled into bed, smiling as Nik Kershaw's **"The Riddle"** made her wonder: *how is it that so often we hear a song that perfectly matches what we're thinking, feeling, or experiencing at that moment in our lives?* She felt that odd connection with this song, relating to the ominous Whitlock Society. She rolled over, and soon Josie drifted into a deep sleep, exhausted from the day's events. As she slept, a dark shadow emerged from the mirror in her room, moved toward the door, and disappeared through it without anyone noticing. The shadows that scare us most appear when we least expect them.

Chapter Thirteen

<u>DON'T FEAR THE REAPER!</u>

Anthony was sound asleep when the alarm clock next to him suddenly went off at an ungodly hour: Blue Öyster Cult's 1976 hit **"(Don't Fear) The Reaper"** blaring in his ear. Shocked and groggy, with his vision still blurred from sleep, he slammed the snooze button and sat up—an evil cackle coming from near the Art Deco club chair in the middle of the room. "Who's there?!" Anthony demanded, fumbling to put on his glasses. But he quickly recognized the sinister chuckle echoing around the room: "Alaric?!" Anthony fumbled and turned on the bedside lamp next to the maroon four-poster bed he was sitting on, to see Alaric standing beside the chair—tall and thin, wearing a wide-brimmed hat and a dark suit, his white, razor-sharp teeth gleaming in the moonlight coming through the French windows. "Hello, Anthony," he said smoothly as he left the chair and walked toward

Anthony, sitting down beside him.

"Wha ... What do you want?" said Anthony in agonizing discomfort, both from Alaric's invasion of his personal space and his frustration at being woken up in such a way and at such an hour. "Now, Anthony, I'm just having a little fun. I bet you didn't know I could channel music, did you?" he said with a wicked, self-satisfied smile. "I could have woken you up by choking you ... would you rather I do *that* next time?" he hissed menacingly. "No ... music is fine, Alaric. What do you want?" Anthony asked, sitting upright in reaction to Alaric's stern, threatening demeanor. "How is my story coming along?" he asked. "Good, good, nearly finished," Anthony nervously assured him.

"Excellent, my boy. Excellent!" Alaric began. "You know that the last few paragraphs must be typed on one of these Whitlock typewriters downstairs in the basement because the magic ink is fresh in those machines. Your typewriter has been battered and bruised and isn't quite working the way it should..." Anthony interrupted Alaric, "Yes, you have already told me this, and so I will have the last page written before I leave the estate. But about your end of the bargain... when will Josie fall in love with me, and when will the horror manuscript I showed you go global?" Anthony quizzed Alaric, who was a little annoyed at the young man's impatience. "My boy, don't you trust me?" he smirked. "All in due time, but first do the work, and you will have all that you desire."

"No, Alaric, I don't trust you. Josie and Blaine told terrible stories about you last night," argued Anthony.

"Yes, those two will be the death of me. I offered Josie the world, but she was too naive to accept it. Now make sure the last page is finished by the end of the retreat, or all hell will break loose!" he snarled, standing abruptly and strutting over to the Art Deco wardrobe before disappearing into the mirror. Anthony breathed a sigh of relief, glad that Alaric was gone and regretting ever getting involved with him. He went to the bathroom, washed his face, grabbed a Stephen King book— *"Misery"*—from his overnight bag, and started reading. It didn't take long for Anthony to fall asleep just as dawn was breaking.

Meanwhile, in Blaine's room …

Josie woke up and snuck into her fiancé's room at 3:25 a.m., nudging him awake. "Blaine, Blaine, we don't have much time to explore the manor." Blaine grimaced and sighed as he woke up. "Okay, Thelma, Fred's on the case," he said, slipping into his jeans, changing his shirt, and pulling on his cherry Docs. "Very funny, Shaggy," she said. Blaine smiled, "I always liked Shaggy; at least he knew how to have fun during an investigation. Do you have Eleanor's key for Room 13?"
"Yes," she replied, fishing it out of her pocket. "We'll start there. Quick, grab the flashlights from the other bag," she instructed Blaine as she headed for the door and waited for him.

Flashlight in hand, wearing his hoodie pulled tight, and a mischievous grin on his face, Blaine whispered one last time— "Are you sure about this?" Josie held up the key, dangling it in front of Blaine's eyes. "Room thirteen. East wing. Eleanor hid something there. Maybe everything." He nodded. "Then let's go exploring."

The oak wood door creaked open with a groan that echoed down the corridor like a warning. Josie flinched. Blaine turned off the flashlight, realizing they'd need to navigate the mansion's passageways by moonlight. They peered around the doorway to make sure the coast was clear, stepped into the hallway... and carefully closed the door behind them.

The mansion was quiet at this hour. Even the wind outside seemed to hold its breath as Josie and Blaine sneaked down the corridor, the brass key cold in her hand. The silence pressed in on them like the walls. The east wing smelled different: mildewed pages, cigar smoke, and a faint, metallic sweetness in the air. The wallpaper peeled away like old skin. Portraits hung at odd angles, their subjects either turned away or their faces... rubbed out. They walked past closed doors. Eleven. Twelve. Then—Room Thirteen! The key slid into the lock as if it had been waiting for years. Josie turned the key; the lock clicked satisfyingly, and pushing the door open, they stepped inside ...

Finding a light switch as soon as they closed the door, they noticed the room was colder than the rest of the house. A single oil lamp sat on a nightstand, still warm, as if someone had just left. The furniture was covered with white sheets, giving the room a ghostly ambiance ... but there was no dust on the sheets. At the far end, a writing desk faced the only window in the room. On it was a black Whitlock typewriter, gleaming despite the gloom. Josie moved carefully toward it, while Blaine stayed by the door. "It's the same model of Whitlock typewriter as the one at Eleanor's home," she whispered. "How many of these types of typewriters are there?" Blaine asked curiously. Josie shrugged, "Looks like quite a few," she said as she reached out to touch the machine.

As soon as her fingers touched the keys ...

Clack!

One key snapped down by itself.

The letter Y ... then a sentence:

```
You found me.
```

Then words flowed across a blank page. Blaine approached Josie, took hold of her hand, and told her to step back from the device. "No, no, no! We're not doing this again, Josie. Get away!" But Josie stayed still, her eyes fixed on the words spilling onto the page right in front of her...

```
You're the one who freed Eleanor and
June, aren't you? They're watching you,
Josie.
```

She staggered back. The typewriter stopped. Blaine firmly grasped her hand. "That's it. We're torching this thing." But something caught Josie's eye — a panel behind the desk, slightly ajar. The wood peeled away, revealing a hollow space in the wall. She gently released Blaine's grip and examined the opening. Inside, she found a stack of pages, burned at the edges, which she pulled out and laid flat on the writing desk beside the typewriter. Blaine moved beside Josie, peering over her shoulder at the pages of script written in Eleanor's handwriting. Among them was an old black-and-white photograph of Eleanor sitting next to a man in his early forties, with a face Blaine recognized all too well. Frozen, he said, "Wait, Josie. That's … *that's my grandfather!*" The typewriter clattered again.

Some legacies never fade — they are handed down from one person to another.

Chapter Fourteen

<u>GHOST IN YOU</u>

Blaine, shocked, motioned for Josie to leave the room. "Let's go back to my room and work this out," he said, clasping her hand and guiding her out, locking the door behind them. They quietly walked back to his room, and once inside, with the door closed, Blaine approached the mirror. "Eleanor?! Eleanor, we need you!" he urged, visibly flustered, turning and pacing the room impatiently. Suddenly, a golden light radiated from the mirror, forming a portal, and Eleanor stepped out, holding a file. The light in the mirror faded and then vanished.

"Why didn't you tell me my grandfather was involved with the Whitlock secret society?" Blaine begged Eleanor. "I wasn't allowed to discuss it until you knew, which is why I gave the key to Josie. Come sit down, both of you, and I will explain ..." Once they settled, Eleanor continued. "There was a reason you were invited to The Whitlock Retreat, Blaine — not because of your relationship with Josie, but because of your heritage. Yes, your mother's father was a dear friend of mine whom I treasured deeply," she admitted. "Hang on..." Blaine interrupted Eleanor, ... "My grandfather left his wife and daughter — my mother — when she was still in her teens. He wasn't a good man!"

"Blaine ... that's what the former Whitlock Society members wanted you to believe. Alaric killed him the same way he did me," she corrected him softly but passionately. "But why?!" Blaine pushed back. "Because he uncovered Alaric's true, nefarious motives for working with the Whitlock Society, and your grandfather was going to stop him once and for all," she revealed.

"Is he trapped in the typewriter in Room 13, just like you were in Haven Cove?" Josie asked, inspired by these new revelations. "Yes, he is, Josie. Thomas wasn't a writer, but he wielded considerable authority in the Whitlock Society. He discovered new talent, organized events, and ensured the Conduits received Whitlock typewriters

to complete the unfinished manuscripts so the souls of their authors could be released," Eleanor explained. "Well, I'll have to get him out!" Josie declared. "You can't," Eleanor countered, "That's not your journey — it's Blaine's."
"What?!" Blaine exclaimed rhetorically. "You heard me, Blaine," Eleanor said confidently yet softly. "Tomorrow night, you'll have the chance to use a Whitlock typewriter to free Thomas."
"But I don't have the gift," Blaine protested. "Oh, but you do, Blaine. Josie will guide you," Eleanor affirmed. "And I will also be with you."

"Eleanor? Is Anthony the new Conduit for Alaric?" asked Josie. "Yes, he is. Anthony is a troubled soul who has been mistreated for being different. Alaric is lying to him. Sadly, he harbors a lot of hate in his heart, which Alaric plans to exploit, and it will be his downfall unless he learns to forgive those who wronged him."
"So, Eleanor, you're saying that Anthony is a future Darth Vader?" Blaine asked with a smirk. Eleanor shook her head. "I guess you could put it that way," she said with a smile. "Well, what do we do about Anthony?" Blaine asked. Eleanor replied, "You can't intervene just yet. When the time is right, you

will know what to do." Turning to Josie, Eleanor handed her a file. "Here, Josie, you need to see this file from the Realm of Light that will explain everything. Many of these transcripts are my own, along with old photos and notes. You should both review this material before tomorrow so that you have the answers you're looking for."

"Thank you so much, Eleanor, for all your help," Josie said sincerely. "You're welcome," she replied with a smile. "I must go—the realm doorway closes at dawn—but I will return tomorrow night." With that, she stood and approached the mirror, where once again, a golden portal appeared. She swiped her hand and stepped through. Josie, holding the file Eleanor gave her, sat back on the bed with Blaine next to her and rifled through Eleanor's notes while Blaine watched eagerly.

"Thomas Whittaker wasn't just your grandfather… he was one of the founders of the Whitlock Society's modern order. He left when he discovered what a reckless group of directors was doing— using Alaric to gain financial wealth and power for themselves. He tried to warn the other society members," said Josie. She started reading a handwritten note from a Whitlock member, turning pale as she did. She looked at Blaine and said, "Sweetheart, you need to hear this," then read the note aloud.

Thomas died after falling in love with a young writer named Eleanor. They both tried to leave the Whitlock Society, but fate had other plans. Neither of them survived.

John McVillar

Whitlock Society, Senior Historian

Clearly shocked by these disturbing revelations, Josie set the note down to comfort Blaine, who looked hollow as the implications sank in. "You mean Eleanor and my grandfather were having an affair? That's sick! He was 15 years older than her!" Blaine protested angrily.
"It seems so, Blaine ... I'm sorry," said Josie, offering him a brief comfort as she wrapped her arms around him before turning back to the notes. Soon, Josie handed him another page from Eleanor's journal, tucked behind the photo she'd previously shown them; a single passage underlined twice. He read it with a good deal of trepidation:

The Whitlock Society values brilliance but has a legacy to maintain. We were told to marry wisely, weave truth into fiction, and protect the ink. However, Thomas disobeyed. He showed me how to twist a lie into reality and make the reader crave more. They will come for Blaine if they suspect his blood still possesses the gift. But I sealed the ink and bound it to something he cannot control.

Eleanor

Josie reread the note, her heart pounding. Blaine had been deeply involved in this story from the start! And what did Eleanor mean by *binding the ink?* As lightning flashed across the room, Josie and Blaine moved to the window just before dawn. A storm was approaching from the sea, with thunder already rumbling above the estate. They looked out over the cliffs; the lightning illuminated the wind tearing through the gnarled, weathered trees, and their hearts brimmed with questions.

The typewriter in Room 13 was waiting. Tomorrow, they'll start the next chapter. But they learned so much tonight. Blaine whispered, "I think this was never just your story, Josie — it's ours." Josie lamented, saying, "You never told me about your grandfather."

"There's not much to tell," Blaine explained. "He disappeared when my mother was in her early teens, and she was told he had deliberately left my mom and grandmother to move to Texas to be with another woman. "Is that the lie the Whitlock Society told your grandmother?" asked Josie. "Yes, but my grandfather reportedly worked for Whitlock Constructions and traveled for work, building high-rises across America. He would send his paychecks home and return every couple of months. My grandmother truly loved him and passed away a bitter old lady, resenting him for leaving her and his daughter."

"But he didn't abandon them, Blaine," Josie said. "Well, we understand that now, but I grew up believing these lies. I had no reason to doubt them; neither did my mom or her mother. We thought the Whitlock Society was telling us the truth. Now we find out that he was cheating on my grandmother with Eleanor! I'm sorry, Josie, but I still see him as a scoundrel for cheating on my grandmother," he said. "You have every right to feel that way, but how would your mother feel knowing he was murdered and didn't abandon her?" Josie asked, reaching out and wrapping her arms around Blaine. "I think my mom is better off not knowing the truth. Sometimes it's best to let sleeping dogs lie." "I guess you're right... But we need to get your grandfather out of that typewriter before we leave the retreat. Anyway, for now, I should head back to my room so we can get some more sleep before the training session," Josie said lovingly.

She gave Blaine a parting kiss and returned to her room, where she lay on her bed and tried to distract herself from the night's chaos by reaching over and pressing play on her bedside cassette player. **"Ghost In You"** by The Psychedelic Furs played as she closed her eyes, and she quickly drifted off to sleep, too exhausted to dream; worn out from sneaking around the house and all the shocking revelations they had uncovered.

Chapter Fifteen

<u>THE REALM OF DREAMS!</u>

By 9 a.m., the young writers had gathered in the ballroom after breakfast. Mr. Franklin, Ms. McBell, and Ms. Alder were also present along with their security team. "Welcome, Whitlock Writers!" Seraphina greeted the group with a triumphant wave. A security guard locked the doors while another used a remote to lower the shutters over the windows, darkening the room. "Please, guests, don't be alarmed," Tyler calmly assured them. "We need to darken the room to give you the proof you need." Josie squeezed Blaine's hand and whispered in his ear, "It's show time!" She smiled, knowing what was coming.

Seraphina moved to the center of the room and pulled out an antique book, then carefully opened it. A gentle breeze filled the space, swirling softly. "Please don't be alarmed. Just watch and wait for the magic to happen," commanded Seraphina. The room was lined with tall, old mirrors. "Please sit on the floor if you can, as the wind will increase," said

Tyler. The security guards stood casually, keeping their distance from others while guarding the main door — not to stop guests from escaping, but to prevent light from contaminating the room. That could fracture the Realm of Light and create a vortex that might collapse time and space on Earth. "Watch the magic," said Seraphina as she placed the book on the floor and stepped back.

Initially, starlight twinkled softly, rippling across the mirrors in a wave-like rhythm. Then, gradually, an image resembling a hologram appeared in the center of the room, showing a scene from Mark Twain's *Adventures of Tom Sawyer,* with Tom and Huck racing toward a riverbank, sliding down a grassy slope, and nearly falling into the cool water below. Josie looked around and saw that the Whitlock Writers' chins were on the ground. Amazed, stunned, and truly inspired, they had become believers.

The scene faded, and Lewis Carroll's *Alice in Wonderland* appeared before them, with Alice falling down a rabbit hole, her face showing fear and trepidation. The scene quickly faded again, revealing an English moor from *Wuthering Heights* by Emily Brontë. As the wind howled over the moor, windowpanes rattled, and Catherine stood in a doorway. The wind wildly tossed her dark brown hair, and her sparkling hazel eyes were intense and radiant. "Heathcliffe," she cried above the roaring wind, "You haunt me when I drive you away." Seraphina stepped forward, and an image rotated around the mirrors in the hall of Catherine on the ground, hysterical, clutching her chest and screaming Heathcliff's name.

The image vanished, and Tyler signaled the guards to lift the shutters, letting in natural light. Now, the mirrors only reflected into the room. The security guards unlocked the doors. "Come, guests, let's head to the parlor and discuss what you just saw," Seraphina beckoned with a wave of her arm. They followed her into the parlor, where refreshments were laid out. The group settled into club chairs and couches: Anthony beside Evie, Josie and Blaine, Silas sitting alone in a corner, Marla between Rowan and Theo on an Art Deco sofa, with the two young men gathered around her, giving the starlet the attention she wanted.

"Well?" asked Seraphina. "What did you think of the Realm of Light?"
"Amazing, absolutely amazing!" declared Evie

excitedly. "I can't believe I got to see the real Catherine. I'm such a Brontë fan," she added, grinning from ear to ear. Marla piped up, "I still think this is a prank for a reality show," which caused Josie to roll her eyes and, under her breath, mutter, "Idiot!" This drew a knowing smile from Blaine. "Well, Marla, my dear," Tyler said, adjusting his 1920s moustache, "It is real, and you all have a big responsibility." He stood beside Seraphina, handing her a Scotch on the rocks. "A little early to be drinking, isn't it?" she whispered. "Whenever you have to deal with a bunch of precocious youngsters, it's a perfect time to have a drink," he responded sarcastically, eliciting a naughty giggle from Seraphina. She loved Tyler's dry wit.

"Excuse me," said Silas. "This can't be real!"
"What?!" Blaine asked, confrontationally. "You have the proof you wanted. Don't you believe what you've just seen?"
"Well, Blaine," Josie interrupted, "A lot of people ridicule me for being a Christian, and Jesus performed miracles among many people, and most didn't believe that the Messiah was standing right in front of them," she said thoughtfully.

"I get it, Josie, but even doubting Thomas believed once he saw Jesus. Anyway, we're not here to have a theological debate," Blaine said, his face reddening with frustration. "Blaine, I'm just using my faith as an example," said Josie, annoyed with Blaine. Marla chimed in, "Well, Josie, I understand you're a person of faith, but many of us have different beliefs than yours," she said, twirling her hair around her fingers. "MARLA!" screamed Josie, "That comment is completely unhelpful. Why are you being so disrespectful and annoying?!"

"ENOUGH!" cried Seraphina. "You will be tested to see if you have the gift. If you don't, you will leave immediately and go back to your lives as before. The gifted will stay and train."
"Are you planning to kill those who don't make it, to silence them?" Evie asked nervously. Marla chuckled, but Anthony replied, saying, "That's a good question."

"Of course not!" remarked Tyler, visibly upset. "We may be a secret society, but we consider life a precious gift from God. We have a code of ethics, you know?" After he finished, he turned to the waitstaff to fetch him another whiskey. "No," laughed Seraphina, "The ones who don't have the gift will find that within minutes of leaving, they will have forgotten everything that happened in the hall, remembering only that they enjoyed the writer's retreat as they happily return to their normal lives."

"But how?" asked Rowan, the son of the Spanish musician, who had been silent until now.
"The Ink," said Tyler. The young writers all pulled faces, puzzled. "The Whitlock ink is magical and wields power over this mansion and everyone in it. It is the ink and the Whitlock typewriters that allow writers to finish the unfinished manuscripts they're given."

"But how is the ink made?" asked Theo. Seraphina rolled her eyes, growing impatient, so Tyler responded. "You don't need to know that Theo. It's the job of the Whitlock Society to provide those two things to our writers — the typewriters and the ink — so they can do their jobs," Tyler said, sounding mildly annoyed and considering another drink to forget the bother.

"Well, we all have our own lives, and maybe some of us don't have time to be part of this superhero troupe," Anthony suggested sarcastically, standing against a wall and looking agitated.

"The Whitlock Society Writers receive an annual payment of $250,000. This payment will continue if you work for us and submit the approved manuscripts to the Realm of Light. Does that sound worth your time, Mr. Temple?" Seraphina asked smugly, clearly growing tired of these cynical young people. Anthony smiled agreeably. "Well, that sounds good to me!" he said enthusiastically, his grin widening ... then narrowing as a thought came to him. "Hang on, what about the Realm of Darkness?"

Tyler responded to the question. "Good question, Mr. Temple. The dark stories are only handled by experienced Whitlock Writers who have worked with us for several years."

"How many Whitlock Writers are there?" asked Josie. "How long is a piece of string?" replied Tyler. We know that thousands worldwide work for other branches of the Whitlock Society. We are not just an American society but an international one," he explained with growing disdain, tiring of the constant questions. Evie giggled, "I'll be rich!" she beamed innocently, clapping her hands like a child. Marla smiled, "I could live comfortably on that amount." Josie and Blaine exchanged knowing, smiling glances, each understanding what the other was thinking. Together, earning half a million dollars annually, they wouldn't need to depend on Blaine's father's money anymore; they would be financially independent.

"Now, now, don't get cocky, Marla. You must pass the test, and when the training is over, *we'll* decide who stays and who goes, okay?" said Seraphina jokingly as she straightened her white linen pantsuit and gestured to the group while addressing them, "Let's all head to the training room in the basement, shall we?" The writers left their empty glasses at the bar and were led out of the room, down a maze of hallways and stairs, unsure whether they were heading toward salvation or ruin.

As Blaine held Josie's hand while they followed the group, he had World Party's **"Ship of Fools"** on his mind, uncertain about what their future as potential Whitlock Society Writers would mean for their relationship. In fact, a hint of apprehension swept over him as he realized this new responsibility could threaten their growing relationship, which they had worked so hard to preserve despite adversity.

Chapter Sixteen

<u>SHIP OF FOOLS</u>

Seraphina and Tyler stopped at a large door deep within the building and turned to face their guests as Tyler placed his hand on the doorknob. Addressing the group, he said, "Ladies and gentlemen—the Whitlock Training Room." He swung the door open and flicked a light switch, causing the fluorescent tube lights to hum and flicker to life, illuminating a classroom-like setting with two rows of desks, each holding identical Whitlock typewriters. The young writers shuffled past Tyler and Seraphina, who beckoned them into the room. "Sit anywhere you want," Seraphina advised reassuringly, and they randomly sat at the desks, facing their hosts who stood near the doorway. Tyler closed the door, revealing a large, mirrored panel attached to its back.

An uncomfortable silence settled as Seraphina and Tyler stood on either side of the mirrored door, smiling at the group with confident expectation.

Suddenly, a spiraling vortex appeared in the mirror, growing brighter and glowing with a golden hue. Without warning, two young men—punk rockers—stepped out of the vortex, their gelled, spiky hair shimmering under the incandescent lights. Their ears, pierced with hoops and studs, reflected flashes of light that signaled youthful nonconformity in the room. They wore tight black jeans that hugged their legs, creating a sharp, edgy silhouette. Their leather jackets—worn yet stylish—were decorated with punk band logos, pins, and badges. One wore a black Dead Kennedys T-shirt; the other, a yellow-and-pink Sex Pistols T-shirt *with "Never Mind the Bollocks"* in black lettering. Each band's statement stretched tightly over their lean frames, their eyes full of mischief. They surveyed the room with a confident, defiant stare.

Tyler introduced them: "My dear guests, may I present to you the Whitlock Boys?" Marla batted her eyelashes flirtatiously, but they ignored her and greeted Tyler and Seraphina warmly, their sharp, clipped English accents showcasing the raw energy of British punk rebellion. Seraphina and Tyler appeared to thank them for a job well done and for their quick response to a growing problem. Turning to the group, one of the Englishmen smiled and said, "So, I see we have new recruits to TORTURE!" Tyler chuckled jovially, but Evie gasped in fear. "Relax, sweetheart ..." he said in his warm Cockney accent, ... "An English joke." Caine, the other Whitlock Boy, leaned toward Marla, "You can just call me The Mirror Man," he winked, and she giggled like a schoolgirl. Josie, recognizing the song title **"Mirror Man"** by the Human League, rolled her eyes and was seen doing so by Darius, who approached her and said, "Ahh, Caine, we have greatness in our midst; this must be Josie Worthington." He extended his hand to her. Josie hesitated, then reached out, and Darius took her hand and gently kissed the back of it.

Blaine suddenly stood up, fists clenched, but Caine stepped in to calm his anger. "Oi! Hang on, soldier. We're just having some fun. Guess you don't get Brit's sense of humor. No harm meant. Relax, mate, alright?" he said smoothly. Turning to Seraphina, Caine shifted gears. "All right, we have a plane to catch," he announced. "Please give my love to Seth. I'm sorry he couldn't make this trip," Seraphina responded sweetly. "Yeah, Seth had something important come up, but he sends his regards," said Darius. The two men nodded toward the door but paused to whisper to Seraphina while staring at Blaine and Josie. Seraphina looked at Blaine, puzzled. "Okay, boys, give my love to Big Ben and, of course, Seth," she said as she hugged them before they left the room.

"You just met The Whitlock Boys, our experienced Conduits from the UK who handle the Realm of Darkness manuscripts," Seraphina announced proudly. Josie quickly asked, "You mean they're the experienced team that completes unfinished horror manuscripts and frees the trapped writers?" Blaine smiled, knowing his fiancée was joking about the jerks. "Exactly, Josie," Seraphina replied, praising her like a proud mother. Tyler quickly added, "Those boys are the best in the business! Now, shall we put you through your paces and see which of you is Whitlock material and who is going home?"

"Please choose a seat behind one of our Whitlock typewriters. Josie and Blaine, I suggest you split up since you're a couple and you'll need to focus," Seraphina implored authoritatively. The group dispersed around the room, and once in position,

Seraphina declared, "You may be seated"—like a matron ordering hospital staff. The young group sat down and waited for further instructions, while Tyler took Seraphina's hand, gently helped her into a chair, and then sat beside her as she made several micro-adjustments to her clothing and limbs to make herself comfortable. She continued, "Beside you are the last chapters of a deceased author's unfinished manuscript. The author will remain anonymous to you. Please read the last chapter for the next twenty minutes without talking. Try to pay attention to details and think about how you would end the chapter." Theo Radcliffe raised his hand like a schoolchild. Tyler rolled his eyes. "Theo, you are 21, not 12 ... Yes, what is it?" he said grumpily.

"Reading the last chapter won't properly conclude the story if you haven't read it from the beginning," remarked Theo. Tyler was impressed. "Why, Theo, that is so very true under normal circumstances, but if you have the Whitlock gift, you'll instinctively know how to end the story without reading it from the beginning because the ink will guide you subconsciously as to how the story should unfold. You are simply the receptor that receives information from the magic ink and processes it manually. Does that make sense?"

"Actually, it does, Mister Franklin," he said with a curious smile. Seraphina picked up a stopwatch and poised her thumb over a large button. "You have twenty minutes, starting NOW!" she said as she pressed the button on the watch. The writers turned to their manuscripts and started reading quietly. Blaine tapped his feet, heard a noise, then looked up to see Seraphina frowning. He mouthed, "Sorry," and kept reading.

After twenty minutes, Seraphina announced, "Time's up, writers! Please turn your manuscripts face down." Tyler rose to address the class. "You will now begin writing automatically, allowing the ink to finish the story as naturally as the original author. You have two hours to write until lunchtime." Heads down, the group started typing. Some machines rattled like machine guns under the hands of their speedy operators, while others clicked more slowly and unevenly, their keys being searched for and poked by two-finger typists. Josie looked up to see stars emerging from the typewriters and circling their heads. She looked down and smiled. This was familiar to her, and she was enjoying every minute of it; others stopped momentarily to gaze open-mouthed at the spectacle ... and the time went by very quickly indeed! Lost in concentration, it seemed like only minutes had passed when Tyler stood up with his hands raised and said, "Well done, Whitlock Writers; you can stop now. It's time for you to return upstairs for lunch while Seraphina and I review your work."

"Review our work? How?" demanded Rowan with his Spanish accent. "You are such an inquisitive boy, Rowan—when you finally speak—good for you!" Tyler said patronizingly, wearing a mocking grin. "But that is for us to know and for you never to find out. Now, OUT!" he barked, losing his patience. Seraphina responded with a witch-like cackle that doubled the writers' eagerness to leave the room, which they quickly did. "Tyler, dear, that was so cruel," she said, smiling knowingly. "I'm sorry, but some of these young writers are just infuriating," he explained. That was the last Josie heard as they made their way back up the winding passageways to the dining room, where they were greeted by Ms. Alder, who led them inside. Blaine plopped down next to Josie. "I can't wait for this bloody weekend to be over!" he exclaimed, sounding like a whiny school kid.

"How did you do?" asked Josie.

"Not good. I'm a fine artist, Josie, not a writer."

"Well, I don't want to be stuck here without you!" she said desperately. "It's Saturday afternoon, and the retreat ends tomorrow."

"So, what if I go home?" he carelessly suggested. "So what? Your memory will be erased!"

"Okay, okay," he said. "I get it. Let's hope I pass." Lunch ended quickly, with everyone lost in thought about their manuscripts; the table was strangely quiet, and the young writers barely looked at each other. After their meal, Ms. Alder led them to Seraphina and Tyler at the landing, tension thickening in the air as each writer prepared to learn their fate.

Seraphina addressed the group. "Now, after the first round, I'm sorry to say ..." Tyler whispered, "I'm not!" She giggled. "Tyler, darling, please behave." He smiled, "Sorry, my love."
"Now, what was I saying?" Seraphina's brow furrowed as she refocused, tilting her head with a gentle smile. "Yes, I'm sorry to say, Marla and Theo, you don't have what it takes to be Whitlock

Society Writers." She shook her head softly, her shoulders sagging slightly.

"Why?" Theo's eyes widened in exaggerated surprise, throwing his hands up enthusiastically. "Because Theo ..." Tyler began, puffing out his chest, ... "Being a rationalist is a serious obstacle to creative writing!" He leaned forward eagerly, voice rising in sincerity to a theatrical pitch. "You see, you must strike a delicate balance. Rational thinking is needed to organize disordered thoughts, but creativity must dance with the chaos, especially in a fantasy world where things that make no sense often make the most sense!" He spread his arms wide like a starfish, grinning mischievously. "Now, Marla ..."

"I don't care, Tyler. I want to escape this hellish place and see my agent for a role that won't involve talking to you!" she snapped; her eyes rolling so much, it's a wonder they didn't pop out of her head. She tugged at the sleeve of her jacket, as if it held the teleportation button she desperately needed. Her voice dripped with sarcasm, and her hand flicked her hair dramatically, emphasizing her impatience. Meanwhile, Tyler watched her theatrics with a bemused grin, arms crossed. The security team arrived, Marla and Theo's luggage in hand, and with a flourish, they guided the pair out through the doors at the grand entrance.

As their feet hit the weathered porch, their faces lit up like kids on Christmas morning, a quiet relief washing over them. Their eyes brightened with a radiant, innocent gleam as they scanned their surroundings. Looking back, they waved enthusiastically to their hosts and the writers behind them on the landing. "Bye, thanks for a fun weekend!" Marla called out cheerfully, Theo joining in, their farewells softly echoing as they left, strolling carefree and unaware of the lingering echoes of the past twenty-four hours. The security personnel carried Marla and Theo's bags behind them, their steps muffled on the pavement as they escorted the departing guests to their cars, hidden behind some bushes in the distance.

"Now that we've taken out the rubbish..." Tyler sneered, ... "Let's talk!" Tyler slammed the door and walked toward the parlor. "I NEED A STIFF DRINK, SERAPHINA!" he called out as he disappeared down a corridor. The group looked dazed and stunned. "Let's go, shall we?" said Seraphina encouragingly, and she led Anthony,

Silas, Evie, Rowan, Josie, and Blaine to the parlor. "Sit down, my lovelies," she said like a serpent. They all sat, and Blaine chuckled, "That was a hoot!" Josie frowned as if scolding a toddler. "Well, it was, Josie!" Blaine complained, wide-eyed and pretending innocence. She tried not to smile, feeling relieved she was finally free of Marla and could breathe again. Once drinks were poured, Tyler proposed a toast: "To the *new* Whitlock Society Writers!" They all raised their glasses and drank to sweet success. "Now, down to business," Seraphina said more seriously. "You all scored about average, but one writer scored exceptionally well." Josie smiled, expecting her to accept the accolade. "Blaine Cordwell, your score is the highest trial result we've ever had." Blaine choked on his drink, and Josie's face turned pale. "What?!" she barked in vexation.

Tyler asked, "Do I detect a pang of envy, Josie Warmington?" Blaine looked at Josie. "Josie, I'm just as surprised as you are." Anthony interrupted, "Well, Blaine, it looks like you're quite a dark horse and full of hidden talents. Congrats." Josie got up to leave, and Blaine grabbed her arm. "Josie, please sit down," he pleaded. He looked at her with puppy-dog eyes, and she realized she was being foolish and that she should be happy for Blaine. "Okay, I'm sorry for reacting as I did..."

"Can we continue this episode of *Days of Our Lives* privately and at your own pace, please?" Tyler quipped. Josie looked at Tyler remorsefully. "Yes, sorry, Tyler," she admitted, eating crow. They sat quietly and attentively, listening to Seraphina explain the next stage of their training. After an hour of discussion, the rest of the afternoon was free for socializing or exploring the Whitlock estate, which included a swimming pool, tennis court, croquet, a hot tub, and stables with horses for riding the extensive grounds.

Late in the day, Josie and Blaine went to their bedrooms. Josie chose a hot, steamy shower to wash away her pride and envy over Blaine's success. As she stepped out of the shower, wrapped in a towel, she passed the mirror above the sink. "Josie Worthington!" a familiar voice called sharply. She wiped the fog from the mirror and saw Eleanor inside a vortex, her expression one of disappointment. "Eleanor?" Josie said, surprised to see her in the bathroom mirror. "Yes, Josie. Get dressed and come back to the bathroom—we need to talk. NOW!" Eleanor demanded in a stern tone that frightened Josie. Josie left the bathroom, dressed, and slowly returned to find Eleanor still waiting in the mirror.

"Josie," she said. "Blaine is not supposed to know this, but he actually failed the test."
"WHAT?!" Josie exclaimed, stunned.
"Josie ... Tyler and Seraphina are scheming, and Blaine's life hangs precariously in the balance," she whispered in a shadowy tone. Josie's face quickly lost its color, draining like ink in water.
"Remember, Josie, always question your assumptions because things are hardly ever as they seem. Blaine must release Thomas in Room 13 at midnight. I'll be waiting in the shadows. Oh, and don't tell Blaine any of this!" she cautioned, vanishing from the mirror like a ghost. A chill ran down Josie's spine, as if someone had stood on her grave; the shadows whispering secrets only she could hear.

Chapter Seventeen

<u>IF YOU WERE HERE</u>

Eleanor moved quietly across the library floor; her footsteps barely audible on the polished wood. She approached Marcus, who was leaning over the circulation desk, his brow furrowed in frustration as he argued with a familiar figure, James Matthew Barrie himself. "You cannot borrow the original manuscript of Peter Pan," Marcus said. "You can't even look at it," Marcus added, growing impatient. "The characters are alive in the archive, floating in the story, and any interruption could destroy them."

The library buzzed around them, with books whispering and pages fluttering, creating a gentle symphony of silent stories. Although some might believe that leisure is the top priority after death, many writers still linger, enjoying their old works and reflecting on their legacies. Barrie, still more boy than man, seemed to embody a gentle yet stubborn spirit. His slim frame barely reached five feet; his shoulders were narrow, and his arms were more delicate than strong. Pale skin, a pointed nose, and thin lips that often twitched into a wry smile characterized his sharp yet inviting features. His deep, haunting eyes—darker than night—seemed to carry the weight of unspoken sorrows, showing that he had aged beyond his years.

His clothes were faded and ill-fitting, making him look like a boy lost in a dream. Ink stains dotted his cuffs, his jacket was worn, and his shoes scuffed from wandering through worlds. When Barrie looked up and saw Eleanor approaching, he blinked with a flicker of irritation. "Can I help you?" he asked softly, his voice carrying a Scottish accent. He often seemed quite preoccupied, as if silencing hushed conversations with unseen friends. Yet, when focused and attentive, his wit shone brightly sharp, quick, and capable of catching others off guard. An otherworldly presence seemed to surround him, as if he was straddling the line between reality and imagination, a feeling intensified by his knack for spinning whimsical tales.

Beneath his shy exterior, a nearly desperate need to create worlds where sorrow is overcome by wonder simmered—this need defined his life's work. "I'm so sorry, Mr. Barrie, I am the Library of Dreams' Chief Editor and Archivist—no writer is permitted to access the special, original manuscripts," she confirmed, flashing her perfect white teeth and flicking her blonde curls. "Well, that isn't acceptable," said James, adjusting his jacket with some agitation. Eleanor cupped her hand near Mr. Barrie's ear and whispered, "I am aware of a lovely Sylvia Plath who is keen to make your acquaintance," she said seductively. All writers who had once passed into the Realm of Light had eternal knowledge about other writers. His cotton cheeks turned red, and he responded, "Well, I do admire this lovely lady's work. A bit morbid, but a talented female author is rare these days," he said, Eleanor, pulling a face.

"Come with me," said Eleanor, wrapping her arm around him, giggling like a schoolgirl, and leading Mr. Barrie to where Sylvia was sitting, deeply engrossed in her book. After a quick introduction, Sylvia was honored to meet James, who sat down beside her, chest puffed out proudly like a rooster parading before a hen. Eleanor smiled, excused herself, and hurried back to the circulation desk.

"Well, I am impressed," said Marcus, praising Eleanor's persuasive skills as he reviewed recent releases. Eleanor smiled, "Yes, you just need to know how to distract these famous authors; they're naturally sensitive about their manuscripts. But I had to laugh at his comment about Plath's work being morbid," she said. Marcus chimed in agreeably, "Is he aware that some literary critics have interpreted Peter Pan as a child serial killer taking the lost boys' lives to keep them young forever?"

"No, I think he would scream blue murder at that bizarre interpretation, and I'll thank you to keep it from him, Marcus—you are never to tell him," Eleanor insisted. "Oh, and Marcus, please make sure you see me after work because I have a surprise for you," she said brightly.

"Okay, I'll do that," Marcus replied as Eleanor hurried toward the archive section of the library. She had spent days searching the Library of Dreams' Irish collection and found Marcus's final work, completed by a Whitlock Conduit. She touched the cover, and it shimmered mysteriously—*A Fool in Love* by Marcus McFarlane.

Eleanor knew she was doing the right thing now that it was confirmed her beloved Thomas was trapped at the Los Angeles Whitlock Retreat. She would soon have the love of her life back. But her feelings for Marcus were tugging at her heartstrings. She lied to him when she said that a writer couldn't live in their story because if all deceased writers knew that they could, how many could resist the temptation? And what would the realms of light and darkness look like then? But Eleanor knew Marcus's book was going to be a wedding present for his fiancée, and so she considered giving him the option to permanently become a character and live forever in the inked pages of his own personal love story. She gently placed the book back on the shelf, noting its location for when Marcus came to see how his fictional life played out.

Eleanor returned to her office and kept herself busy until Marcus knocked on the door. "You have a surprise for me?" he asked. "Yes, I definitely do!" she replied, leaving her desk. She stepped out of the room, took Marcus's hand, and immediately felt a surge of excitement run through her veins. "Where are we going?" he asked innocently as they descended a flight of stairs into a restricted area housing the archival repository. "I found the unfinished manuscript you were working on when you died: '*A Fool in Love,*'" she explained, motioning him into a large room lined with bookshelves. "You found it?" Marcus asked excitedly. "You mean …?"

"Yes, Marcus," she replied, "We're going to see how your story ends—how the Conduit finished it." She gently took the book, moved it to a table oddly placed in front of a large mirror, and set it beneath the mirror. "How does this work?" Marcus asked eagerly. "You'll see," she said as she opened the book. Light immediately streamed from the mirror. With a burst of air swirling around them, a golden, spiraling portal appeared, shimmering like sunlight. "Are you ready?" asked Eleanor, her hair blowing in the wind as she took his hand. "More than ready!" Marcus eagerly confirmed, and they stepped into the mirror, disappearing.

Marcus and Eleanor found themselves in pre-war Dublin, standing outside a small café on O'Connell Street, where the cobblestone was slick and shiny from the rain that had just fallen, reflecting the gaslit streetlamps and twinkling like stars. With World War looming, the ongoing economic depression had families waiting in line for dinner at a nearby soup kitchen, and decaying posters peeling off brick walls. Lively young men in uniform approached them on foot, animated with anticipation about their upcoming adventures abroad, naively unaware of the horrors of war. Marcus's main character, Private Michael Callahan, was among them. "Can he see us?" Marcus asked excitedly. "No," whispered Eleanor, "We are like ghosts in this literary world. He will even walk through us," she said as the attractive young man tugged at his hat, being polite to a woman with a pram as he passed through Eleanor and Marcus as if they weren't there, and then the young soldiers ducked into the cafeteria.

The brass bell above the café's entrance door chimed, and the scent of boiled tea and scones, along with the soft hum of conversation, filled the air. Michael moved toward the counter where a girl in a bright yellow dress stood with her apron snugly tied around her waist. She seemed to be in her late teens, with stray rose-gold curls framing her cheeks that had fallen loose from the bun holding most of her hair. Her eyes, as green as Wicklow fields, sparkled and caught the gaslight streaming through the cafeteria's glass windows.

Private Callahan froze, mesmerized not only by her beauty but also by her kindness to her customers. The sound of the kettle boiling and spoons stirring the teacups all faded as he looked at this beautiful girl. "Tea, soldier?" she asked softly. He nodded slightly. "Yes, please, a strong cup of tea is just what I need right now," he said, fumbling to gather coins from his pocket. She noticed his hands trembling, gently touched his arm, and smiled. "It's okay, soldier. No need to be nervous. I can tell you have a kind heart, so I'm going to give you one of my homemade scones for free, with a big dollop of cream and freshly made strawberry jam."

"Why, thank you," said Michael as she hurried off to fill his order. Marcus and Eleanor watched. "So, what's going to happen now?" Eleanor asked softly, breaking Marcus's focus on the scene, his written words playing out before him like a movie in a theater. "Her name is Catherine," he said. "She is my fiancée in ink; the character is based entirely on Clara—and this girl even looks exactly like her," he whispered, lost in wonder. Eleanor and Marcus remained invisible to the characters in the story as they watched the narrative unfold for the man behind the ink.

"My name is Catherine," the waitress said as she returned with a cup of tea and a scone. She extended her hand, which the soldier gently took and kissed, causing a giggle from Catherine, who admired his chivalry. The café was busy, so she left him awkwardly. The silver bell above the door jingled, welcoming more customers, while Michael sat at the café counter, watching Catherine warmly greet new customers, occasionally giving him an encouraging sideways glance and smile, sometimes giggling.

After pouring more tea for the elderly couple, she returned to Michael and squeezed his hand. A wave of heat surged through his body, emanating from his pounding heart. Catherine had brown freckles like constellations across her nose and cheeks, and her ruby-red lipstick stirred in him an urge to embrace and kiss her passionately, right in front of all her customers... but he restrained himself, locking the encounter away in his memory for inspiration and comfort on the battlefield. "I told you my name is Catherine, but everyone calls me Clara," she said, "But you haven't told me your name?"

"I'm Private Michael Callahan, and I'm very glad to meet you, Clara," he formally introduced himself. "When are you leaving, Michael?" she asked as she moved up to the counter to serve an elderly man. Michael swallowed hard. "Tomorrow morning. I leave on the train," he said sadly. She stepped closer and whispered in his ear, "Sometimes we need to grab life with both hands ... I finish work in half an hour, and I would love for you to walk me home along the river, if you'd like."
"I would be delighted!" he responded unreservedly. She pulled back to examine his blue eyes as he confirmed, "I would love to escort you on a summer evening stroll, Clara!" The faint scent of her lavender soap tantalized his senses. "I'll wait until you finish work," he added with a smile. "It's a date!" Clara concluded and scampered into the kitchen.

Eleanor looked at Marcus. "Tell me about your fiancé?" she asked warmly. "Clara and I were high school sweethearts. We met in English class and became inseparable. We were both accepted into the same college, but she didn't want to be an author; she had a gift for editing that she wanted to pursue. If only I had canceled that meeting with my publicist— it was a stormy night, and driving conditions were terrible. If only …" Marcus lamented, choking up as tears filled his eyes. Eleanor held his hands firmly. "Marcus?" she said, drawing his attention. "What if I told you that you could stay here?" Marcus looked at Eleanor, his brow furrowed with confusion. "What do you mean, Eleanor?" he asked. "What if you could replace yourself and become Private Michael Callahan?" she explained. Marcus still looked confused. "Eleanor, you told me we shouldn't interact with our own creations—that doing so would have disastrous consequences."

"Marcus, if an author *is* the main character, then they can become part of their own story. I see how much you still love Clara, and here she is, in this literary world you created as a wedding gift to her! You can take back your life with her and live it out together as you intended," she said. A fire blazed in Marcus's eyes. "But Eleanor ..."

"Marcus, think about those annoying writers in the Realm of Light. Do you really want to deal with them forever?" she teased with a wry smile. "When you put it that way..." he said with a chuckle. "But what about Alaric? You need help to defeat him," he added. "Already taken care of!" she reassured him. "A good friend will be joining me soon at the Realm of Light, and he knows how to handle Alaric." Eleanor paused for a moment, gathering her thoughts.

"My sweet assistant and friend," she began, "If I had the chance to reunite with my soulmate, I would seize that opportunity with both hands and all the strength I have. Please don't let this offer to start over pass you by. What happened to you was tragic. But now you can take your rightful place in your own love story," she pleaded. After careful thought, Marcus simply said, "I'm going to miss you, Ellie," as he squeezed her hands tightly.

"I'll miss you too, Marcus," she said with a mixture of sadness and happiness, knowing this was the right choice for her heartbroken assistant. "So, what happens next?" he asked eagerly. "You just walk over to Private Callahan, touch his hand, and you will become him in the story you created and relive your romance with Clara for all eternity," she explained.

"Eleanor, you said a Conduit finished the story. Is there a happy ending?" Smiling, Eleanor said, "The first thing I did was check the ending. Yes, Marcus, you and Clara marry, have children, and live a wonderful life together filled with love, song, and happiness!" Marcus smiled and stood up to hug Eleanor tightly. He whispered in her ear, "You know you are a wonderfully generous and selfless person for doing this, and I am grateful for this amazing gift." He kissed her softly on the forehead.

A wave of conviction swept over Eleanor, and she reassured herself that she was letting Marcus go into his own creation out of her love for Thomas. She cared deeply for Marcus, but now that she knew where Thomas was, she planned to free him with Blaine's help. *Marcus is a good man who deserves a second chance at true love with Clara,* she told herself. She also faced a harsh blow from fate, but she was determined to reunite with the only man she had ever loved. Eleanor looked up and said, "Goodbye, Marcus. I'll miss you."

Marcus gazed longingly into Eleanor's eyes, smiled, then turned and walked directly to Private Callahan. He looked back at Eleanor one last time and said, "Goodbye, Eleanor," before touching Callahan's arm. A faint glow appeared around Marcus and Michael that only she could see, then Marcus dissolved right into Private Callahan, and the Marcus she knew was gone.

Eleanor wiped tears from her cheeks as she watched Clara and Michael for a moment, reassuring herself that Marcus was a lasting part of his own love story. Private Callahan and Clara walked out of the cafeteria, laughing as they cheerfully strolled down the rain-slicked cobblestone path. Eleanor stood outside the café for a little while, watching the couple stop, embrace, and share a kiss for the first time, silhouetted against the evening sky. Eleanor smiled warmly. Her work here was done, and she could head home to the Realm of Light.

Walking in the opposite direction down O'Connell Street, Eleanor looked for a shop window. Spotting a cake shop around the corner, she closed her eyes, focused, and softly moved her hand across the reflective glass.

Light appeared, shining brightly, as she turned to give Marcus's world one last look, then stepped through the portal, determined to create her own happy ending with Thomas.

Chapter Eighteen

<u>THE UNGUARDED MOMENT</u>

Josie disliked keeping secrets from Blaine. He failed the test, but she didn't want to burst his bubble, so she kept Eleanor's revelation to herself while they spent the evening watching TV and playing Chinese checkers in her room. Tired of distractions, Blaine cuddled Josie, his long hair falling loosely on her cheek just as The Church's **"Unguarded Moment"** played on Blaine's mixtape. He smiled; this Australian band had a significant influence on him, and he made a mental note to discuss The Church with Evie—their new Australian friend—tomorrow.

Meanwhile, Josie was enjoying Blaine's touch; her first true love's embrace still felt electric and filled with excitement, it was sensually thrilling... and soon they would be getting married. Blaine grabbed a hairbrush and began singing along to the song, serenading her. She sat up, clapped her hands, laughed at his antics, then eagerly took the hairbrush from him, tossed it aside, and jumped on top of Blaine, kissing him passionately.

Rain began falling outside as he ran his hand down her back, making her feel like the only girl in his world. Catching his breath, he softly whispered, "Josie, you saved my life. Until I met you, I wasn't truly living, but you have a way of making everything worth it. I love you, future Missus Cordwell." Tears filled Josie's eyes; her heartbeat matched the rhythm of the music. "I love you too," she whispered, kissing him as they had at first— sensual, raw, and with unreserved honesty.

The evening grew late, and as Blaine prepared to leave, they agreed to meet again, just like the night before, and sneak back to Room 13. This time, their goal was to free Thomas. After catching his breath, Blaine checked the time and saw it was 2:53 a.m.; Josie was hovering over him in the dark, shaking him awake. "Good morning!" she said sarcastically, grinning in the dark and now pulling Blaine out of bed. "Okay, okay, I'm up. Lemme get dressed," he said, pushing himself up and reaching for his clothes, Dr. Martens, and flashlights.

He dressed quickly, and as they moved toward the door, he said, "Well, my love, it's time for me to meet my philandering grandfather," grinning derisively. "Come on, you don't know the full story," Josie countered. He slowly opened the door, making sure it creaked as little as possible, then gently closed it behind them with the same care.

"Do you have the key?" he asked Josie.
"Right here in my jacket pocket," she said as he took her hand, and they quietly tiptoed down the long corridor toward the east wing. Art deco lights flickered dimly on both sides of the hallway, seeming like an omen of what was to come. They noticed the lights were still on in Evie's room and could hear a TV softly humming in the background, along with loud snoring. Blaine smiled and whispered, "Who would have thought a girl that cute could sound like a freight train when she sleeps?"

"Blaine?!—be nice!" Josie smirked.
"I'm just saying ..." Blaine rolled his eyes, acting innocent. "SSHH!" Josie warned, "Someone's coming!"
"Quick," said Blaine, pulling Josie into a utility closet filled with brooms and mops. They could

hear heavy footsteps and the clicking of high heels. "Mrs. Delver," Josie whispered. They held their breaths as they heard her pass and go up another flight of stairs in the distance. Blaine cautiously opened the door and, peeking down the corridor, whispered, "The coast is clear, Velma." "Thanks, Shaggy," said Josie, smiling. They moved carefully, stepping softly on the creaky old wooden floor to avoid making too much noise. They turned a corner, and an Art Deco clam light above a doorway barely lit their destination— "Room 13," whispered Josie. She pulled out the vintage key and gently unlocked the door.

The room was musty, with old newspaper archives on the coffee table. Blaine turned on the light as they entered, and almost instantly, an amber flash lit the adjacent ensuite briefly before Eleanor stepped out, wearing a beautiful '70s-style sundress. Her hair was pinned up, with ringlets loosely framing her face. She had paired her retro dress with pale peach lipstick. "You look gorgeous, Eleanor!" Josie complimented her, realizing she had dressed especially for this occasion. "Well, being reunited with your one true love is a special event," Eleanor explained, smiling nervously.

Blaine glared at her angrily, however. "You mean adulteress!" he snapped sharply. "Hey!" Josie stepped in to defend Eleanor. "No, Josie, it's okay. Blaine is right. Please come and sit next to me," she said. "I need to explain our situation." Blaine hesitated, but Josie gave him a look that demanded he show some compassion. He approached and sat on a chair opposite Eleanor and Josie.

I was twenty-two when the Whitlock Society brought me on as one of its newest writers. I was young and naïve, and at first, I didn't believe in myself. But it was Thomas—your grandfather, Blaine—who made me realize how powerful storytelling can be. Authors create worlds where people can escape, and that's something special. Your grandmother Vivienne was a lovely woman, and he cared for her deeply. He never planned to leave her, and I never planned to give him up either," she said.

Blaine leaned forward slightly, his eyes searching her face for a reaction as he asked, "Did my grandmother know about you?" His voice trembled with curiosity, sounding almost tentative. She nodded gently, the gesture subtle but deliberate. "Yes, she did ..." she replied softly, her fingers tracing an invisible pattern on the table. ... "But they agreed to stay married, and she chose to ignore his indiscretions." Blaine hesitated, running a hand through his hair, then pressed on, "What about my mom? She was a teenager when he vanished. Did she know?" Eleanor's eyes lowered with sadness, and she shook her head slowly, her shoulders sagging. "No, Blaine. She didn't," she said quietly, her voice barely above a whisper, "And that was the way Vivienne and Thomas wanted it. They fell out of love long before I met your grandfather; their fire had burned out many years ago," she lamented.

"Eleanor, do you mind if I ask who died first? You or Thomas?" asked Josie curiously. "I did, Josie," Eleanor answered, her voice cracked and raspy. "As soon as the waves tore my body apart, my soul was instantly trapped in the Whitlock typewriter in Haven Cove. A few days went by, and Thomas confronted Alaric on the cliff top about my disappearance. Well, Alaric used the same solution on him as he did on me. His spirit was immediately transported and trapped in one of the typewriters at the Whitlock Estate in Los Angeles. We were separated by death, but I never stopped loving him," she said, wiping tears from her cheeks.

She glanced at her watch under the dim Art Deco lights, pressed her lips tightly, and said, "It's time!"—nervously. They all stood up, and Eleanor confided in the couple, "I'm so nervous!"

"Okay, so Eleanor, what do I need to do?" asked Blaine. She moved to the window near the writers' desk and pulled back the curtains, revealing a full moon, sparkling from the recent rain and shining through onto the typewriter.

She placed a sheet of crisp white paper into the carriage, rolled it onto the platen, snapped the paper bail in place, and stepped away. "Sit at the typewriter, please," she instructed Blaine, who went to the desk, pulled out the chair, and sat comfortably in front of the typewriter. "Now we wait," she said. Josie and Blaine briefly exchanged nervous glances. "Look!" Josie exclaimed as a ghostly mist appeared around the typewriter, illuminated by an amber light emanating from within the machine. "Place your hands gently on the keys and start typing as you feel led, Blaine," she whispered, holding Josie back as she moved closer to see better. "Please stand back," said Eleanor, smiling excitedly.

"You can do this, Blaine," said Josie. "I believe in you!" Blaine looked nervous, but hearing Josie's confidence in his abilities encouraged him to close his eyes, place his calloused, guitar-playing fingertips on the keys, and start typing. At first, the typing was slow and hesitant, but the speed increased as Blaine imagined what a world without Josie would be like. And so, he wrote to his grandfather:

```
I never truly understood what love was
until I met Josie. Before her, I
drifted through life alone, fighting my
inner demons. Alcohol, drugs, and a
dark, restless craving for death
haunted every step I took. But
everything changed the moment I reached
Haven Cove. That's when I finally saw
myself as Josie saw me—not just Blaine
Cordwell, the son of a rockstar—but
Blaine: a soul ignited by love, beauty,
and music.

I discovered my true passion, my
heart's melody, in painting the world
of my dreams, my love, and my very
soul. With each stroke of oil on
canvas, I expressed the love that Josie
awakened in me—a love that tugged at my
```

heartstrings and made me feel alive for the first time.

What I'm trying to say, Grandpa, is that I have finally grasped the true meaning of love, and with a compassionate and sincere heart, I forgive you. I forgive you on behalf of my mother and my grandmother Vivienne, whose spirit still lingers in the whispers of the wind. I forgive you because when you find your soulmate, it's as if the universe itself conspired to bring you together in an unbreakable bond. You cling fiercely, hand in hand, facing fear with unwavering courage, inviting radiant joy into your life.

My deepest wish is for you and Eleanor to be surrounded by love so pure that it lights up the stars. I know my mother would feel the same; her love for you still shines brightly in the memories we cherish. So, Thomas, I send you off with an open heart into our world—a world of endless possibilities—so that you may love and be loved, as we all deserve.
Your Grandson, Blaine.

As Blaine finished the last word, his hands started to shake; the desk trembled, and a bright blue light erupted from the typewriter. The window suddenly swung open, sending a gust of wind into the room and making papers fly everywhere. "IT'S WORKING!" Eleanor exclaimed excitedly, grabbing Josie's arm. The light hovered over the typewriter; Blaine blinked hard to clear his vision and widened his eyes, mesmerized as an apparition began to form, settling in front of the desk and gradually materializing into a man in his early forties. A handsome, older, mustached version of Blaine, dressed in a brown suit with a tie and his hair gelled back. He looked around the room dazedly, a smile spreading across his face as he fixed his gaze on Eleanor.

"Hello, Thomas," she said, smiling brightly. "Is it really you?" asked Thomas as he approached and embraced her, then lifted and twirled Eleanor around. Hearing the commotion, Blaine opened his eyes to see his grandfather passionately kissing Eleanor. He carefully got up from his chair, trying not to interrupt the reunion, and put his arm around Josie. He smiled, glowing with satisfaction and wonder. Josie kissed him on the cheek. "You did really well, sweetheart," she said, and for the first time in a long time, Blaine was speechless as he watched the long-lost lovers reunite. Thomas eventually looked around, focusing on Blaine and Josie, his face lighting up with recognition. "Do I know you?" he asked, puzzled.

"Thomas, may I introduce you to Blaine, your grandson?" Eleanor said. "Grandson? My goodness! I have been gone a long time, haven't I?" He walked over, smiling broadly with outstretched arms; he said, "Give me a hug..." then pulled Blaine in close, not letting go for a long moment. "Let me look at you," he said, finally breaking the embrace. "I can see you take after me. Is your mom here?" he asked, looking around quickly. "No, she's not," Blaine replied sadly. Eleanor awkwardly added, "I'll fill you in later, Thomas," and continued, "This is Josie, Blaine's fiancée," and he warmly embraced her. "Honored to meet you, sir," Josie said, and they exchanged pleasantries. After a brief chat, Eleanor explained she needed to take Thomas to the Realm of Light.

They said their goodbyes, promising to meet again soon, and as they left, Eleanor whispered, "Thank you," to Blaine over her shoulder before leading Thomas to the ensuite. mirror.

Josie and Blaine, eager to see their departure, approached the doorway just in time to watch Eleanor wave her hand in the mirror to open the portal. "After you, my love," she said sweetly to Thomas. He smiled, but before stepping through, he turned once more to Blaine. "I know your mother would be very proud of what you did here today," he said, smiling. "We'll catch up soon," he assured Blaine, waving goodbye. Blaine nodded with a smile in acknowledgment.

Eleanor and Thomas stepped through the mirror into the Realm of Light—lovers reunited and eager to make up for lost time. The light in the mirror faded, and they disappeared. "Wow!" said Josie, stunned by what they had just seen. "That was awesome!" she added. "Yeah, it was," Blaine agreed enthusiastically, wrapping his arms around her and kissing her. "I love you, Josie, and I always will," he said. As he kissed her, Josie remembered Eleanor's warning about Blaine being in danger.

She was suddenly overwhelmed with a terrible urgency to get him out of the room as quickly as possible. "Let's get out of here and go back to our rooms before Ms. Alder catches us," she said. Blaine hurriedly followed Josie through the door, and she gently closed and locked it behind them. As they walked back down the hallways to their room, arm in arm, they were unaware of a noise coming from Room 13. The Whitlock typewriter started making noise. CLICK, CLACK, CLICK, CLACK ...

Lovers might be reunited in death, but Blaine, your love for Josie will face a test before sunset tomorrow...

ALARIC

Chapter Nineteen

<u>DECEPTION</u>

Meanwhile, 12:30 a.m. at the Whitlock Estate's basement training room ...

Anthony entered the training room and was surprised to see Silas standing in the middle, smiling. "I've been waiting for you, you're late," he said in his thick French accent. Anthony asked, "What are you doing here?"

"Let's just say Alaric wanted to make sure you didn't screw this up," said Silas as he took off his jacket and sat at a desk. Perplexed, Anthony approached Silas. "You know Alaric?" he asked, placing a manuscript beside a Whitlock typewriter across from Silas. "Let's just say we go way back," replied Silas with a smirk.

"Now, shut up, and let's get this done," he demanded. Anthony sat down, put on his glasses, and carefully took the manuscript out of its leather-bound satchel. "Place the last page in the typewriter and hurry," Silas urged, glancing around nervously. Anthony followed orders, then looked to Silas for more instructions. "What do we do now?" he asked. "We wait," Silas replied. The young men sat patiently for a while, and just as Anthony began to think this was all a big waste of time, a ghostly white smoke rose from the typewriter in front of him. "It's starting. Place your hands on the typewriter, close your eyes, and type," whispered Silas, standing over Anthony and watching eagerly. Anthony did as he was told and soon saw a ghostly figure flicker in front of his desk. He hesitated.

"WRITE THE BLOODY ENDING!" yelled Silas. With his eyes closed, Anthony began pounding the keys—his fingers moving on their own.

```
The writer slouches at his cluttered
desk, shadows flickering across his
face as he ponders his uncertain
future. Did he stumble? Perhaps. The
lure of quick success is a shimmering
promise that temptingly dances before
his eyes, too alluring for a battered
soul to resist. I crave fame, power,
and riches—he quietly admits to
himself—as memories of relentless
childhood torment echo in his mind,
```

tearing at his confidence and leaving scars that no words can heal.

Since youth, he endured the cruel jabs and cold neglect of his peers, each wound fueling his desperate need for recognition and acceptance—or escape. In the shadowy corners of the schoolyard, he often lay battered and bruised, not just by fists but by the relentless sting of being different. He was a delicate soul, slammed by worldly brutality, clutching a book while the ruffians chased football in the dust. The scars of his sensitivity lingered, making him a target for mockery and humiliation by the school jocks, who reveled in his suffering. The pain of rejection seeped deep into his bones: a reminder that being true to himself came with a high cost.

Yet, amid this darkness, he now stood tall; the torment he endured awakened him to the truth that he had the power to overcome his past. I am no longer a victim; I reclaim my strength to heal what was broken. I will take control of my life: right here, right now! Alaric is taking charge of his destiny. Today,

I take command of mine...

As Anthony typed the last word, a misty figure shrouded in blue light started to materialize from the apparition that had first appeared. Silas smiled. "You did it, Anthony! Open your eyes!" Anthony opened his eyes to see a younger Alaric standing before him — in his late 40s — still wearing a black trench coat, with the same dark, coal-like eyes and razor-sharp teeth. "YOU DID IT, MY BOY, YOU DID IT!" Alaric exclaimed excitedly. Suddenly, a woman's scream pierced the air, and Anthony turned to see Seraphina and Tyler standing in the open doorway.

"YOU STUPID BOY! WHAT HAVE YOU DONE?!" roared Tyler. Seraphina quickly grabbed a bottle of Whitlock ink and handed it to Tyler, who ran and poured the magical ink onto Alaric, creating a bloody-looking mess that dripped down Alaric's face. He immediately screamed in pain.

Anthony stepped back, unsure of what to do as Silas tried to escape but was stopped by two Whitlock security guards at the door, preventing him from leaving the room. "We don't have much time, Tyler," said Seraphina as she ran to the typewriter, noticing the ink still shimmered wet; she set fire to the page. Screaming in terror, Anthony watched himself catch fire, too. Tyler grabbed a fire extinguisher and sprayed Anthony as he collapsed on the floor, unconscious and writhing in pain.

Alaric also collapsed to the ground as Seraphina closed her eyes, waved her hand, and a cage appeared around him, trapping him with Whitlock Ink's powerful magic. The cage bars shimmered with bright light as Alaric lost consciousness. Silas, still in the custody of the Whitlock security team, was led downstairs to a holding cell while protesting his innocence. Anthony was severely burned, and the security guards called the resident nurse to come and treat him. He was quickly moved to the infirmary in the mansion's east wing.

Once the chaos had settled, Seraphina wiped her face and fixed her hair. Tyler approached and embraced her. "Quick thinking, my love," he said while kissing her forehead. "Do you think Anthony is going to make it?" she asked, looking distressed. Tyler looked at Seraphina with affection. "You know this was part of the test, don't you?"

"I know, Tyler, but sometimes I wonder..." she responded sadly. "Settle down, my love," he said softly, placing a gentle finger on her lips. "Our son will be fine, and the ink will restore him to normal; it just takes time for him to heal. The first lesson an author learns is that writing can heal old wounds, but first, you need to have the scars." Then he looked at Seraphina. "You know I still see the young Realm of Light writer I fell in love with many years ago," he whispered in her ear before slowly pressing his lips softly against hers with a calming, healing kiss. Love can heal all wounds, but you need to open your heart to receive it.

Chapter Twenty

<u>HIDDEN SECRETS</u>

Josie blinked awake as the morning sun's bright, golden rays streamed through the windows. She stirred and looked around the room, startled to see Eleanor standing at the foot of the bed. What was more unsettling was that she looked visibly shaken. Rubbing the sleep from her eyes, Josie pushed herself up on one elbow. "Eleanor?! What's going on?" her voice now thick with concern. "Something bad ...?" Josie added, feeling a sinking wave of dread wash over her. Eleanor stood stiffly in her sharply tailored pantsuit; her hair pulled back into a severe bun that emphasized her stern expression. The sight unsettled Josie because she had never seen Eleanor like this before.

A gentle knock at the door broke the silence. It was Blaine. Eleanor let him in, but the smile on his face quickly disappeared when he saw the heaviness on both Eleanor's and Josie's faces. Josie sat up, and

Blaine took her hand as Eleanor finally said, "I'm so sorry to wake you, but something happened last night while we were freeing Thomas," she said anxiously. "What happened, Eleanor?" Josie leaned forward, growing more alarmed. "Anthony released Alaric in the Whitlock Training Room last night!" Eleanor confided, shaking her head. Josie's face drained of color, her eyes widening in shock. "But don't worry," she hurriedly added, her voice trembling slightly, "Seraphina and Tyler handled the situation, and they've imprisoned Alaric and Silas in the basement."

"WHAT? SILAS? What does he have to do with this?!" Josie exclaimed, her voice rising in exasperation. "Silas was working for Alaric, who sent him to the writers' retreat to ensure Anthony materialized him," Eleanor explained succinctly. Blaine's eyes widened and blinked quickly with growing outrage. "Where's Anthony?!" he demanded, fists clenching at his sides. "I'm going to thump him," he muttered through gritted teeth, the muscles in his jaw tightening as he prepared to move.

Anthony sustained serious burns and lacerations from the ordeal and is unconscious, but he's being treated by Whitlock medical staff at the infirmary in the east wing," Eleanor responded. "They have their own hospital here?" Blaine blurted out absent-mindedly, only to be met with a stern look of disapproval from Josie. "Yes, Blaine. There's a small medical unit on the grounds at these retreats in case anyone gets hurt," Eleanor said, rolling her eyes as she sat on the bed. "This is all my fault," she lamented. "How can any of this be your fault?" Josie asked dismissively. "I was too focused on freeing Thomas," Eleanor admitted, "I didn't even consider Alaric being released."

"Eleanor," said Blaine, grabbing her attention. "Josie and I both know this isn't your fault, and Anthony is the one responsible, and it sounds like he is paying the price for his stupidity."
"BLAINE!" Josie barked. "It sounds like you're glad that Anthony is really hurt!" Josie said sternly. "GOOD!" he said smugly. Eleanor looked solemnly at Blaine, "Now I know you don't mean that, Blaine, and you'll be pleased to know the Whitlock medical team is competent."

"I can't believe you said that about Anthony," Josie cried, dismayed. "I'm sorry, Josie. I know he's your friend, but we've been trying to get rid of Alaric, and this guy is helping him!" Blaine countered sharply. Eleanor placed her hands on both Josie and Blaine's shoulders. "Listen, I didn't come here to have you quarreling. I just wanted to inform you of the situation... But now I must get back to Thomas, as he is still adjusting to the Realm of Light," she said with a smile.

"So, how is my long-lost grandfather this morning?" Blaine asked. Eleanor smiled, "Thomas is good and sends his regards to both of you," she affirmed as she stood up. "So, Josie, your intuition about Silas was right. Always follow your instincts; they will never lead you astray." At the full-length mirror, Eleanor raised her hand, and a shimmer of gold appeared. "Take care, you two," she said, turning to face them briefly; then she turned back to the vortex into which she stepped and disappeared.

Josie sat on the bed with her arms crossed, feeling angry at Blaine. "Sometimes I feel like I don't know who you are!" she declared, sounding upset. Blaine crawled over to her side of the bed and wrapped his arms and legs around her. "Yes, you do," he whispered in her ear as he kissed her neck. Josie smiled and turned so his lips brushed hers. Sometimes, the best way to resolve an argument is with kisses rather than words.

There was tension at the breakfast table, with only Josie, Blaine, Rowan, and Evie present. Seraphina quickly addressed the issue. "Writers, Anthony and Silas, have left the program and won't be continuing," she said, turning to Tyler to continue. "Both Silas and Anthony left early this morning, leaving a note saying they were no longer interested in the Whitlock writing opportunity. They were escorted out by security at dawn. I can see that you're upset, but this means we can spend more time with each of you before you leave this afternoon," he said. "We wanted to reward you for making it through the trial session yesterday, so let's finish breakfast quickly," Seraphina suggested, starting on her French toast.

Evie's face twisted with deep distress, her eyes desperately scanning the room as if trying to see beyond what was visible. "I'm sure Anthony will contact you ..." Josie whispered almost inaudibly, her face filled with concern. Evie finished her toast and tea, trembling with worry. "That's not why I'm upset, Josie," she whispered hoarsely. "They didn't leave, Josie; they are still here. I can feel Anthony's presence, and it's like a cold, jagged knife slicing through my chest. Anthony is badly hurt, wounded, or trapped somewhere in this suffocating, oppressive prison. We're being deceived, Josie. I can feel his torment, his agony, lingering in the shadows." Her voice cracked, raw with primal fear. Josie, knowing the horrific truth about Anthony and what had happened to him the previous night, immediately looked away, and her own fear for Blaine's safety now gnawed at her, overshadowing everything else.

Chapter Twenty-One

<u>REAL WILD CHILD</u>

Anthony lay unconscious, covered in burns. Seraphina sat beside him, clutching his hand. She felt terrible that he had to endure this final test to determine if he would eventually join The Whitlock Boys as a Realm of Darkness writer. She looked at his severely burned face, which was slowly healing thanks to the essence of Whitlock ink routinely applied to his wounds.

His heart monitor remained steady, and his breathing stayed normal. He was in a dreamlike state, his eyes flickering beneath his closed eyelids. Seraphina reflected on how dangerous it could be to interact with spiritual beings, and how, like Anthony, many writers before him had faced similar risks. She looked at Anthony's face, loosely framed by his light blonde hair. Confident in his healing abilities, she noticed he was growing stubble, which would soon require shaving.

Anthony sensed someone nearby, but he assumed it was Josie, his only friend in the world. He was walking through a field filled with daisies and flowers from around the world, blooming in full splendor—the scent and colors were invigorating. As he moved across the field, he felt happy, and for the first time in his life, completely carefree! He saw the outline of a young woman on the other side of the field, slowly walking toward him and waving.

He couldn't initially tell who it was, but as he approached her and the gap between them narrowed, his face lit up when he recognized her, and he shouted, "JOSIE!" She waved back and started running as fast as she could toward him, her curled dark hair with crimson red highlights cascading around her shoulders. With superhuman strength, he bounded toward her, speeding up as he took deep breaths of clean air, his nostrils filling with the wonderful scent of blooming spring.

Josie laughed gleefully as he picked her up during their embrace and twirled her around like lovers in a romantic French movie. Setting her down, she smiled at him with pure joy. "Josie! What are you doing here?" he asked excitedly. "You tell me,

Anthony; it's your dream," she answered coyly as his hand brushed her face. He leaned in as Josie tilted her head upward to receive his kiss. Passion ignited, and he felt a pure love unlike anything he'd felt before.

Suddenly, the sky darkened, and lightning flashed all around them. They didn't move, remaining mesmerized by that first kiss. "Josie?" Anthony murmured as Seraphina held his hand. She was a little surprised, but now she understood that a love triangle existed between Anthony, Josie, and Blaine. She rubbed his hand. "Anthony," she said soothingly. "You're safe and recovering well," she assured her son as he murmured Josie's name again. "Hush now," Seraphina said, "sleep, sweetheart, sleep." Anthony smiled and drifted back into his dreamlike state, where he and Josie continued in the throes of mutual love.

Seraphina checked her watch and realized the last training session for the Whitlock Retreat was about to begin. She tidied the covers over Anthony and gently kissed his forehead before leaving the room. A nurse at the door, who had come to check on Anthony, greeted her. Seraphina walked down the hallway, through the automatic double doors, and used a security key on a keypad to keep the sick bay private from curious visitors. She briskly moved through the long, winding hallways and stairs back to the training room, where Tyler was waiting impatiently with the other writers and, of course, the Whitlock security personnel.

"I'm so sorry for being late, and I apologize profusely for my tardiness," she said as she entered the room. "Come sit by a Whitlock typewriter, any typewriter," she casually suggested. While the trainees found their chairs, Tyler whispered in her ear, "Seraphina, darling, I know you were visiting Anthony, but please don't get emotionally attached. He may be our long-lost son, but he remains oblivious to the fact that we are his birth parents," he said, his voice thick with emotion.

"I know," Seraphina responded softly, a mix of frustration and longing in her eyes. "Please don't lecture me, Tyler. You know the Whitlock Society made me put him up for adoption, and now that I have him back in my life, you're not going to interfere."

"Seraphina, you know I adore you, and I'm genuinely glad to have Anthony back myself, but he's a strong candidate to work with the Whitlock Boys," Tyler said, hopeful yet concerned.

"I know, Tyler. Please stop lecturing me!" she snapped sharply, a flicker of defiance crossing her face. She looked away, her chest rising and falling as she composed herself. Josie sat two typewriters away from Blaine, attentive but distant; the rest of the group filled the room with murmurs, each carrying their own unspoken burdens.

"Welcome, Whitlock Writers, to your final training session before you return home," she said. "Today, we will work on a manuscript from a real writer in need of your help. The writers will stay anonymous, but they are all deceased, and their souls are stuck in limbo because of their unfinished work. They cannot enter the Realm of Light until their stories are completed and released," she said. "Just like yesterday, you now have twenty minutes to read the last words of the author's story, let it sink in, and then you'll have the rest of the morning to finish the story and let it go to its own world, freeing the author," she said dramatically, raising her hands in a grand gesture.

Josie was still upset with Blaine's attitude toward Anthony and glanced at him as he was immersed in his manuscript, casually yawning, which amused her greatly and made her smirk. She turned her attention to her unfinished work and read, absorbing the words. Evie and Rowan were lost in their own worlds, and Evie's expressions told her she was in the writer's zone, fully engaged in the story and immersed in the world of writing. "Okay, writers," said Tyler after twenty minutes, "Let's go and free some trapped souls today!" he said inspiringly, like a football coach rallying his team to victory. "Seraphina, shall we have some music for this magical moment?"

"Why not, Tyler," she said as she approached a stereo in the corner and pressed play on the cassette deck, whereupon "**Compulsion**" by Martin Gore blared from the speakers. Josie smiled; music always speaks to her soul. She turned to look at Blaine, who was grinning from ear to ear, and mouthed, 'I L O V E Y O U' at her. Josie responded in kind, then placed her hands on the typewriter keys, closed her eyes, and let the music finish her writer's story.

Tyler and Seraphina sat in their chairs at the front of the room, watching as the writer's hands began to move slowly at first, then in sync with the music.

"Impressive," said Seraphina with a smile as she saw Tyler's frown turn into a grin. "Yes, very impressive indeed." The room was sealed off from outside light because it was in the basement, but just then, something magical happened—something Seraphina had never seen before. Rays of colored light started shining from each Whitlock typewriter, and diamond-like stars appeared, dazzling and swirling beautifully around the room. *"Incredible!"* gasped Seraphina, "That has never happened before!" as the tiny lights swirled around their heads and danced to the music.

"Writers, keep your eyes closed, you're doing great. Let the music help you finish your author's story," Tyler addressed the class warmly. The scene resembled a sparkling forest at night, with fireflies dancing and creating beautiful patterns of light as they fluttered about. Tyler shouted, "Five minutes left, writers!" His voice rang with anticipation. "Bring the story HOME!" The room buzzed with frenetic energy as the writers' hands moved with urgency, now fueled by the pulsating rhythm of Iggy Pop's **"Real Wild Child"** blasting on the stereo. The thunderous drumbeat seemed to ignite their spirits, pushing them to write faster and harder.

Suddenly, Seraphina sprang to her feet, her eyes shining with wild excitement. She twirled into an energetic dance, her arms slicing through the air, her hips swaying wildly to the relentless beat. Her movements were fierce and free, a burst of pure, electric energy lighting up the room. Tyler grinned widely, captivated by her lively display, a spark of joy flickering in his eyes.

He called out, "Finish the last paragraph, writers ..." just as Seraphina struck a dramatic pose, sweat shining on her brow. The atmosphere crackled with anticipation. Then, with a thunderous cry, Tyler declared, "TIME'S UP!" as the song ended, and he turned off the stereo. The room erupted in applause and cheers, the energy still buzzing in the air. Their faces were full of awe and wonder. Tyler walked over to a lever and said, "Now, my prestigious Whitlock Writers, watch the real magic."

He pulled a lever down, and the mirrors on the surrounding walls absorbed the words, transforming them into images. Each glass mirror told a different story: the first showed a mother and child reuniting with laughter. The second depicted a soldier returning home from World War II, greeted by his girlfriend at a train station. The third mirror illustrated a field filled with flowers, where two lovers danced among the spring blooms. The last panel, which was Josie's story, showed a woman giving birth and holding her baby for the first time. Her husband kissed her with admiration for the new life God had created and given to them.

"Good job, writers!" said Seraphina, congratulating them while catching her breath. "Good job ... the manuscripts are now finished and have been released into the Realm of Light, and the written characters will live out their own stories for all eternity." Blaine got up and went to Josie, taking her hand. She was still looking at the mirrors. "This is the most amazing thing I have ever seen, Blaine. Look at how a simple story from a writer's imagination becomes real," she said. Blaine smiled and, in his usual deadpan fashion, said, "Yep, Josie; it looks like I am a writer and a painter all at once." She smiled, looked at him, and said, "You certainly are!"

Tyler then pulled the lever up, and the windows into the Realm of Light closed. It had received the new stories for Eleanor to shelve, and their authors had also entered the Writers' Realm—that part of heaven just for writers. The mirrors returned to normal, and the air was filled with positivity. Seraphina couldn't resist showering the group with praise. "That was the most amazing writing session we have ever witnessed at the Whitlock Estate," she said, excitedly clapping her hands.

Soon, Tyler and Seraphina escorted the young writers out of the training room, locked the door, and led them down the long halls, up the winding staircase to the main foyer. Ms. Alder approached Tyler and Seraphina, whispered something to them, then returned to the library. The group of young writers was excited about what they had created and seen, and they released it into the Realm of Light. Josie, Blaine, Evie, and Rowan were busily chatting when Seraphina politely interrupted.

Well, my young writers, due to unforeseen circumstances, we will be ending The Whitlock Writers' Retreat earlier than planned. It has been a wonderful success, but unfortunately, we must now ask you to pack your bags and leave the estate, she said. Normally, Tyler and I would spend the rest of the afternoon with all of you, but we have urgent matters to attend to. Yes, writers, it is midday, but I know some of you have a long journey home, so maybe it's for the best.

Disappointment and confusion quickly appeared on the young writers' faces. Blaine said what they were all thinking: "So you're kicking us out—just like that?" Seraphina chuckled, "No, Blaine, our formal training program is finished, and you are now one of our Whitlock Writers. You're welcome to stay for lunch. Feel free to use the sauna or tennis court; it's entirely your choice, but the formal part of the retreat is over. An administrative assistant will contact you in the next few days to handle the paperwork, including your bank and tax details, so that you can be properly paid for this weekend's work."

"Excuse me?" Rowan interrupted. "Are we just supposed to go back to our normal lives as if nothing happened?"

"Why, yes, my boy! That's exactly what you are supposed to do. Since you have been chosen, when you leave this estate, you will remember everything — but you mustn't tell anyone what you've seen here," explained Tyler, smiling. "You are now employees of the prestigious Whitlock Society, which means you are sworn to secrecy about our activities here. We will contact you when unfinished manuscripts arrive, and we need a talented writer to complete them." He clapped his hands. "You will be paid monthly, and your wages will be roughly $250,000 a year to be on-call for us whenever needed."

"My dear writers," said Seraphina. "We will stay in touch. And thank you—what you all created this weekend was magical. Rowan, I was especially impressed by your work yesterday, and I'm sure many Spanish manuscripts will need to be finished in the future." Rowan smiled and thanked Seraphina before turning to Evie, who had an idea. "Josie and Blaine," said Evie sweetly, "Would you like to play a game of tennis with Rowan and me?"

Josie looked at Blaine and understood that Blaine wanted to get home to see his father. "Thanks, guys, but we have to head back because Blaine's dad is very ill, and we want to spend time with him if that's okay," she said. Blaine let out a sigh of relief, knowing they could finally leave and put this Whitlock business behind them for a while.

However, he also relished the thought of no longer relying on his father's wealth. Working for the Whitlock Society will give them the financial security and independence they need to build a future as a married couple, buy a house, and raise a family.

Seraphina and Tyler said goodbye to the small group. "We have important business to attend to, so we have to say farewell, and we are so proud of the standards of this year's recruits," said Seraphina, hugging each of them in turn: Evie, Rowan, Josie, and Blaine. Tyler shook hands with Blaine and Roman and kissed Josie and Evie on the cheek before walking down a corridor, chatting with each other until they disappeared.

Blaine turned to Josie and shouted playfully, "Last one to get packed is a rotten egg!" as he sprinted up the stairs, yelling "Goodbye!" to Evie and Rowan. Josie quickly apologized for Blaine's childish behavior and said farewell to the tennis players... then playfully rushed after Blaine, shouting, "That's not fair! You had a head start!" Josie briefly opened Blaine's door to see him rushing to stuff everything out of the drawers into his duffel bag at lightning speed.

She went to her room, grabbed her bag, and burst into hysterical laughter as she hurriedly shoved her clothes into it. She carefully packed the portable cassette player, took out the mixtape she had made for him, and put it in her pocket—thinking it was perfect for the long car ride home. Before long, Blaine appeared behind her. "I WIN!" he shouted triumphantly, playfully grabbing Josie and kissing her on the cheek. "Ready?" he asked. They quickly looked around their rooms to see if they missed anything, and once satisfied, Blaine said, "Let's get out of here. I'm craving a Big Mac!" Josie again rolled her eyes, wrapped her arm around Blaine, and they left their rooms to go downstairs to the car.

Meanwhile, on the South Balcony

Seraphina and Tyler sat on the patio with drinks and a light lunch. Ms. Alder had told them that the Whitlock Society management team would call them for an urgent phone meeting about Anthony's medical status and their serious concerns regarding his eligibility to work with The Whitlock Boys. Seraphina and Tyler wanted Anthony as far from

Alaric as possible, and they agreed the best solution was to move him to the UK to work with The Whitlock Boys so they could keep an eye on him. They watched Josie and Blaine from the balcony, arm in arm, walking toward their car. Seraphina held up her drink while observing them. "Isn't young love grand?" she said. Tyler, also watching, agreed. "Yes, it is, my love," as he took a sip of his scotch. Seraphina sipped her martini and adjusted her sunglasses so Tyler could see her eyes. "Is everything set?" she asked.

"Yes, Seraphina, the final test for Josie and Blaine is about to begin," he said, grinning mischievously at Blaine and Josie as they hopped into Blaine's car, which soon roared to life, backed up, and slowly made its way down the long driveway toward the front gates. "It's a shame, really," Seraphina said sadly, "That we have to do this." Tyler interrupted her, "Now, Seraphina, you're getting sentimental with age. You know grief has a way of making a Whitlock writer outstanding in their profession."

"I know, Tyler," said Seraphina, "But they are such a beautiful couple," she added, growing melancholy. "Seraphina," Tyler began, "We went through the same thing thirty years ago, and it made us stronger. We became better writers, and our romance flourished," he said, motioning toward her. "We need to go to the basement because we have unfinished business before that important phone call." They left their empty glasses and half-eaten meals on the balcony and disappeared through the French doors.

Chapter Twenty-Two

<u>CUTS YOU UP!</u>

Seraphina and Tyler descended the winding staircase to the basement, walking past the training room to the end of the corridor, then entering a code to access a highly restricted area. They passed through sliding doors into a space filled with cell rooms guarded by security personnel. Tyler politely said, "John, we need some privacy to interrogate our prisoners before transportation. Will you and your men give us some time alone?" The guard nodded and led the three large men out of the area.

Tyler and Seraphina approached the cells where Silas and Alaric sat on the floor. Silas looked up with a smile. "About bloody time, I'm starving!" he complained. His French accent had disappeared, replaced by a British one. Seraphina smiled and clapped her hands. "Well done! I think this was the performance of a lifetime," she said. Alaric stood up, no longer wearing his mean, evil demeanor. "So, bangers and mash ready then?"

"As requested," said Tyler with a big smile. "You can change back now," he added. Suddenly, a shimmering gold light passed over Alaric's and Silas's bodies, revealing their true selves. There, in each cell, stood the Whitlock Boys: Seth and Caine. Seth had transformed his appearance into a fictitious writer named Silas to help Anthony pass his writer's test and become a new Whitlock Boy. Caine and Darius lied to the group of young writers in the training room about Seth's location when they claimed he was in the UK.

It took some time for Seth and Caine to feel like themselves again. Seraphina pressed a button, and the cells' gates opened, releasing the boys. Stepping out of his prison cell, Caine asked, "Where's Darius?"

"He's upstairs waiting for you two to have lunch with him," explained Tyler. "Hey, Tyler, what about the guards? They're going to go nuts when they see the empty cells," remarked Seth, the youngest Whitlock boy. Standing at five feet nine inches and in his early twenties, he possessed ash-blonde hair with twisting corkscrew curls that casually tumbled down the back of his neck, catching the light with every movement. "Yes, they will, but we made sure that Cook placed something in their breakfast this morning to make them forget what happened," Seraphina smiled wryly, like the cat who caught the canary.

"You think of everything, Seraphina," Seth said with a chuckle as he walked over to give her a big hug. Seraphina had known the boys for many years and considered them like her own sons. She whispered in Seth's ear, "Thank you for helping our son." Seth hugged Seraphina tighter and responded with a big smile, "You know you're like a second mom to us. It was my pleasure to do this for you, Seraphina." She felt relieved that Anthony's testing was finally over.

"Did Blaine release Thomas from the Whitlock typewriter in room thirteen?" inquired Caine. Tyler smiled mischievously. "Oh yes! Just as expected. That's why he was here in the first place. We couldn't let that poor old chap stay trapped in that bloody typewriter forever," he chuckled, and Seraphina smiled at his witty sense of humor.

Seth changed the subject: "How's Anthony doing?" he asked. Tyler's smile faded as he looked sternly at Seraphina to ensure she remained professional and kept her emotional attachment to Anthony in check. "He will be in the infirmary for another week, but he is expected to make a full recovery, thanks to the power of the ink."

"So, I guess we need to hang around, hey Caine?" said Seth with a smile. "We might do some touristy stuff, eh?!" Caine suggested excitedly.

"Are you sure you secured Alaric in the Realm of Darkness?" asked Seraphina with seriousness.

"Yeah, he'll be released in 48 hours," said Caine. "You know he's going to be mad when he finds out he was impersonated," he remembered, laughing at Alaric's protests when they imprisoned him. "Well, he shouldn't have gone after our son," said Tyler.

"About that... does he know?" asked Seth.
"OF COURSE NOT!" Seraphina sharply rebuked him. "He is never to know, boys!" she said passionately as Tyler nodded in agreement.

"Okay, okay, you're the boss," Caine said, raising his hands. "But just out of curiosity, what does head management think about all this?" Seth asked again. "The powers that be gave us the strict rule that he must be tested and, if considered suitable because of his interest in the horror genre—and the fact that we have passed our writing genes onto him—he is to be trained by you lovely boys in the UK," said Tyler.

"Come, let's go upstairs," said Seraphina, motioning for the boys to follow Tyler and leave the containment area. "What about security?" chuckled Seth. "They should be unconscious by now and wake up with no memory that Silas and Alaric were ever imprisoned," responded Tyler as he hit the keypad, causing the glass doors to open. Sure enough, the three security guards were passed out on the floor. "That is so cool," said Caine as he carefully stepped over the sleeping giants. "Yes, good old Cook knows how to send a man to sleep," Tyler quipped. Seraphina burst out laughing. "Oh, you are *so* naughty, Tyler!" she said, smiling with adoring bemusement as the Whitlock Boys, Seraphina, and Tyler walked through the winding corridors and upstairs to the bar for a stiff drink, where Caine and Seth were reunited with Darius and enjoyed lunch together in the parlor.

Meanwhile, Josie and Blaine were driving down the long, winding mountain road heading back to Los Angeles ...

The windows were open, and the cool air felt refreshing on their faces—Peter Murphy's **"Cuts You Up"** playing on the car stereo. Josie and Blaine were just so happy to be free and away from the stifling oppression at the Whitlock Estate. "You know, Josie," Blaine said, turning to her, "Tyler and Seraphina are actually quite nice—for a pair of upper-class snobs." She smiled, since Blaine's bluntness was one of his most endearing qualities. "Yes, they are okay in small doses," Josie agreed, enjoying the beautiful mountain views from the steep incline off the road. "You know, Josie, I'm glad we went," said Blaine with a big smile, continually turning to look at her. "BLAINE, KEEP YOUR EYES ON THE ROAD," barked Josie. "Okay, sorry, Josie," he said, then refocused on driving. There was so much to see on the trip home, and Blaine's mixtape, which Josie made especially for him, was great to listen to as they sang along loudly.

"Echo and the Bunnymen's "**Bring on the Dancing Horses**" came on, and Blaine made sure to turn it up loud. Josie was excited to get back home — yes, Blaine's home was now her home, and his family was her family, knowing they'd be married soon. She could hardly wait, and since they wanted Blaine's father at their wedding, it would have to happen soon, as time was running out with Dean's terminal lung cancer. Blaine's mom, Grace, approached them promptly after his marriage proposal to Josie to discuss their wedding plans and start organizing the big day.

Josie was going dress shopping with Grace next week, and they planned to visit wedding reception venues the weekend after. Josie reflected on a year ago when she was alone in Haven Cove, surrounded by her '80s alternative music and her writing. Now, she was a Whitlock Writer studying journalism and engaged to such a wonderful person who was amazing inside and out. Josie began drifting off to sleep, wearied by the winding roads. She could hear "**Human**" by The Human League, lulling her to sleep.

Suddenly—the loud screech of skidding tires and the car lurching violently to the left—she opened her eyes wide to see a deer in the middle of the road. Blaine avoided hitting the animal, but as he veered off the road, the car flipped over the embankment, rolled three times, and landed on its roof; smoke billowed from the engine.

"BLAINE!" she screamed, her voice cracking like shattered glass as she desperately tried to free her left arm, her trembling fingers clutching his blood-soaked shoulder. She shook him gently, hope flickering like a fragile flame as he lay motionless and made no sound. No response—the silence was heavy and unforgiving. She clutched her chest, her heartbeat pounding in her ears. Nothing. The car grew silent, and so did she, desperate to hear anything from Blaine. She caught a faint echo of a shallow, rattling breath from Blaine, which sounded haunting and dark, then nothing at all, just silence. "BLAINE, BLAINE!" she cried hysterically, tears streaming down her face like icy rivers, "DON'T YOU DARE LEAVE ME NOW!!"

Her body shook as she broke down, sobs of grief escaping from the crash. Outside the crushed vehicle, muffled voices of a man and a woman drifted through the cracked windows, words meaningless to her swirling mind as she hovered on the edge of consciousness, caught between life and death.

"Blaine?" she whispered, her voice trembling as she heard the distant wail of sirens growing louder, the sound slicing through the air like a razor. Pain burned through her, sharp and relentless, as her eyes fluttered closed and she slipped into a dark abyss. The paramedics' voices blended into a soothing hum as they carefully lifted Blaine out of the driver's seat, the glow of flashing lights flickering on shattered glass. She faintly heard the rhythmic pounding of CPR being performed on Blaine, a fragile symphony of desperation. Finally, her world faded into silence, her senses slipping away as a haunting melody played on the somehow still working stereo. Joy Division's "**Atmosphere**" was seeping from Blaine's car stereo, a ghostly dirge as she drifted into unconsciousness.

Blaine stood before an ethereal, alabaster library that seemed to glow with divine light, its walls shimmering like an angel's wings. Behind him, his grandfather Thomas and Eleanor stood, their faces etched with sorrow, their eyes glistening with tears. Blaine hesitated, then stepped forward, voice trembling. "What am I doing here?" he whispered, desperation creeping into his tone. Eleanor moved closer, her arms trembling as she pulled him into a fragile, hope-filled embrace. "Sweetheart, I'm sorry you didn't make it," she whispered, her voice breaking. Blaine's eyes burned with agony as he shouted, "NO ELEANOR! DO SOMETHING! I CAN'T LEAVE JOSIE THIS WAY! HER PAIN WILL TEAR HER APART!" his voice cracked as he turned to his grandfather, who stepped into his embrace, offering silent comfort. Blaine collapsed into sobs, the weight of despair crushing his heart as he begged for a second chance. Hot tears streaming down his face—his hopes and dreams for a life with Josie, shattered like broken glass.

To be continued … mid-2026

Author's Note

Thank you so much for reading the sequel to *Sincerely Yours... Written In The Stars And Inked In Destiny!* The final book in this series will be out in July 2026, revealing the fate of our beloved '80s couple, Josie and Blaine. I must admit, it will be tough to write the last book, as I have fallen in love with these two young people who have overcome adversity to be together.

I am an author dedicated to writing exclusively for children and teenagers with disabilities. My husband, who is an editor, supports me in this endeavor. Together, we handle all aspects of our writing independently. You can help spread the word about my work with children with disabilities, especially those with ASD, by subscribing to my social media channels and following my posts. My passion for writing and the joy I get from it are advantages.

If you enjoyed this book, please check out my other works, including my autobiography, *The Crazy Mother's Guide To Raising Exceptional Children,* which shares my family's personal story. Warning: You'll need a good sense of humor to read it. I encourage you, as a reader, to take a few minutes to visit the links on the next page and leave a review. Why? Reviews not only help me improve my work but also motivate others to read the novel. I don't have a marketing team—just my faith, my love for writing, my amazing husband, and the wonderful supporters I mentioned in the acknowledgments.

The following links will direct you to where you can leave a brief review if you'd like to share your thoughts with other potential readers. Stay tuned for the final book in the series... Trust me, it'll be well worth the wait!
God bless,
Sonia D. Hebdon

Review Links

U.S

Amazon

https://www.amazon.com/stores/author/B0DTJCFM3P

Good Reads

https://www.goodreads.com/author/show/54141309.Sonia_D_Hebdon

Barnes & Noble

https://www.barnesandnoble.com/s/sincerely%20yours%20written%20in%20the%20stars%20and%20inked%20in%20destiny

U.K

Amazon UK https://www.amazon.co.uk/Sincerely-Yours-Written-stars-Destiny/dp/1764105605

Waterstones https://www.waterstones.com/book/sincerely-yours-written-in-the-stars-and-inked-in-destiny-book-1/sonia-d-hebdon/adam-e-marshall/9781764105606

Blackwell's UK

https://blackwells.co.uk/bookshop/product/Sincerely-Yours-Written-In-The-Stars-And-Inked-In-Destiny-Book-1-by-Sonia-D-Hebdon-author-Adam-E-Marshall-editor/9781764105606

Hive.co.UK https://www.hive.co.uk/Product/Sonia-D-Hebdon/Sincerely-YoursWritten-In-The-Stars-And-Inked-In-Destiny-/32125965

AbeBooks https://www.abebooks.co.uk/9781764105606/Sincerely-Yours-Written-stars-Inked-1764105605/plp

AUS
Amazon AUS
https://www.amazon.com.au/stores/Sonia-D.-Hebdon/author/B0DTJCFM3P?

Booktopia
https://www.booktopia.com.au/search?productType=917504&keywords=Sincerely%20Yours...Written%20In%20The%20Stars%20And%20Inked%20In%20Destiny

Angus & Robertson.
https://www.angusrobertson.com.au/books/sincerely-yourswritten-in-the-stars-and-inked-in-destiny-book-1-sonia-d-hebdon/p/9781764105606

Google Books
https://www.google.com.au/books/edition/Sincerely_Yours/N_Jf0QEACAAJ?hl=en

Kogan
https://www.kogan.com/au/buy/the-nile-sincerely-yourswritten-in-the-stars-and-inked-in-destiny-book-1-9781764105606/

Canada
https://www.amazon.ca/Sincerely-Yours-Written-stars-Destiny/dp/1764105605

Social Media

https://soniadhebdonbooks.com

https://www.facebook.com/profile.php?id=61569399597133

https://x.com/hebdond53953

https://www.tiktok.com/@soniad.hebdon1

YouTube

Book Trailers for all of Sonia's works can be found here:

https://www.youtube.com/@SoniaD.52

Music Reference List

Altered Images (1981). I CAN BE HAPPY [Song]. On PINKY BLUE. Epic Records. (UK).

Blue Öyster Cult (1976). DON'T FEAR THE REAPER [Song]. On AGENTS OF FORTUNE. Colombia Records.

Depeche Mode (1987). BEHIND THE WHEEL [Song]. On MUSIC FOR THE MASSES. Mute Records.

Echo & The Bunnymen (1985). BRING ON THE DANCING HORSES [Song]. On SONGS TO LEARN AND SING. Korova.

Eurythmics (1983). SWEET DREAMS (Are Made of This) [Song]. On SWEET DREAMS ARE MADE OF THIS. RCA Records.

Fiction Factory (1983). (FEELS LIKE) HEAVEN [Song]. THROW THE WARPED WHEEL OUT. CBS.

Joy Division (1980). ATMOSPHERE [Song]. On B-Side, TRANSMISSION. Factory Records.

Iggy Pop (1986). REAL WILD CHILD (WILD ONE) [Song]. On BLAH -BLAH -BLAH. A&M Records.

Martin Gore (1989). COMPULSION [Song]. On COUNTERFEIT EP. Mute Records.

Modern English (1982). I MELT WITH YOU [Song]. On AFTER THE SNOW. 4AD-Sire.

Nik Kershaw (1984). THE RIDDLE [Song]. On THE RIDDLE. MCA Records.

Peter Murphy (1989). CUTS YOU UP [Song]. On DEEP. Atlantic Records US.

REM (1987). IT'S THE END OF THE WORLD AS WE KNOW IT (AND I FEEL FINE) [Song]. On DOCUMENT. I.R.S Label.

The Cure (1989). LOVESONG [Song]. On DISINTEGRATION. Fiction Records.

The Go-Go's (1984). HEAD OVER HEELS [Song]. On TALK SHOW. I.R.S Label.

The Human League (1986). HUMAN [Song]. On CRASH. Virgin, A&M.

The Human League (1982). THE MIRROR MAN [Song]. On B-side, YOU REMIND ME OF GOLD. Virgin Records.

The Jesus and Mary Chain (1989). HALFWAY TO CRAZY [Song]. On AUTOMATIC. Blanco y Negro Records.

The Psychedelic Furs (1984). GHOST IN YOU [Song]. On MIRROR MOVES. Colombia Records.

The Psychedelic Furs (1987). HEARTBREAK BEAT [Song]. On MIDNIGHT TO MIDNIGHT. Colombia Records.

The Thompson Twins (1983). IF YOU WERE HERE [Song]. On QUICK STEP & SIDE KICK. ARISTA

Records.

Wang Chung (1984). DANCE HALL DAYS [Song]. On POINTS ON THE CURVE. Geffen Records.

When In Rome (1987). THE PROMISE [Song]. on WHEN IN ROME. Virgin UK.

World Party (1986). SHIP OF FOOLS [Song]. on PRIVATE REVOLUTION, Chrysalis & Ensign Records.

ABOUT THE AUTHOR

Sonia D. Hebdon is an Australian author who shares a love story like Blaine and Josie's with her husband. As a former Goth during her college years, she enjoyed '80s alternative music. She holds a degree in Creative Writing and Communications from the University of Western Sydney, where she met her husband, Adam.

Sonia is a Christian author from Australia who is passionate about raising awareness of Autism and Dissociative Identity Disorder because of her own experience raising children with disabilities. She aims to make a positive impact on the writing industry by featuring main characters with well-known disabilities in her stories.

Additionally, all her work is in large print, with a minimum font size of 16 points, shorter paragraphs, illustrations when possible, and plenty of white space. Over the years, she has learned that these subtle changes help children with ASD, ADHD, and many other learning disorders process written information better.